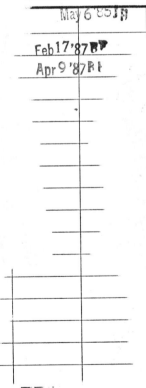

Pieface and Daphne

Pamela Teitelbaum, otherwise known as Pieface, is an only child and used to being the center of attention. When her fourth grade class experiments with cutting down on TV viewing and substituting a new interest, Pamela decides that her new activity has to be the most unusual. So she befriends Shirley Brummage, an independent old woman who collects junk, and soon she and Shirley are going on daily rounds together.

Conflicts develop though, when Pamela's mother decides to have Daphne, a troubled 11½-year-old relative, come to stay. "It's so you'll get the feeling of what it's like to have a sister," her mother explains. Pamela, unused to sharing the limelight, resents Daphne whose strange, dreamy ways seem to arouse sympathy from Pamela's family and especially her doting grandmother. But most infuriating to Pamela is the strong attachment that the tough, eccentric Shirley seems to feel for Daphne.

Tension continues to mount between Pieface and Daphne until a crisis involving Shirley casts both girls in new roles. By the end of the story Pamela has begun to part company with the "me" generation, making a decision that proves she is capable of sharing—or at least negotiating.

Young readers will identify with both Pieface and Daphne, as Lila Perl brings humor and insight to a lively, well paced-story.

Pieface and Daphne

Lila Perl

PIEFACE
and
DAPHNE

 Houghton Mifflin/Clarion Books/New York

Cover Illustration by Bernie Colonna

Houghton Mifflin/Clarion Books
52 Vanderbilt Ave., New York, NY 10017
Copyright © 1980 by Lila Perl
All rights reserved. No part of this book may be
reproduced or transmitted in any form or by any means,
electronic or mechanical, including photocopying,
recording or by any information storage and retrieval
system, without permission in writing from the publisher.
Printed in the United States of America

Library of Congress Cataloging in Publication Data

Perl, Lila.   Pieface and Daphne.

Summary: When Daphne comes to visit Pamela
and the two cousins become involved with a shopping
bag lady, Pamela becomes less self-centered.
[1. Selfishness—Fiction. 2. Cousins—Fiction]
I. Title.   PZ7.P432Pi   [Fic]   79-23815   ISBN 0-395-29105-4

1 "Pamela, what was that deafening noise?" That was my mother yelling from downstairs. She was trying to yell quietly.

My mother and my father and I—*especially* I—were supposed to be very quiet because Grandma Florence was staying at our house since her latest operation.

"My schoolbooks," I answered in a whispery croak that made me start coughing. "They s-s-slid off"—cough-cough—"my bed."

"Pamela Ann Teitelbaum," my mother demanded, "get down here this minute."

I went padding down to the kitchen in my socks. My mother was standing over a soup pot in a cloud of steam. I stood there with my arms folded, waiting.

"Here am I," she said, half talking to herself, "trying to make matzoh balls the way *she* does. If they're not light as a feather, your father will call them cannonballs, and . . ."

She turned to look at me and we both started laughing, our hands quickly covering our mouths.

I love my mother. Really. Maybe it's because

1

we look alike—small and sort of pudgy, with round faces and shining thick dark hair. We even have the same haircut, short all around with a heavy fringe across our foreheads. And when we laugh our eyes crinkle up exactly the same way.

But lately my mother was getting so moody and picky.

She put the last matzoh ball into the pot and sat down at the kitchen table, stretching her legs and turning her toes inward, which meant her feet were tired.

"Now really, Pammy, we've got to talk about this. No kidding."

"I didn't wake her up," I protested. "If I did, you know she'd be calling out by now: 'Eh-veh-lyn, Eh-veh-lyn.' "

"Pam! Don't make fun. How can you? She's your Grandma. The only one you have." My mom sighed. Her own mother was dead a long time. Grandma Florence was my father's mother.

"She loves you. You know that."

"I know." I thought of all the kisses on the top of my head and the hugs that pulled me tightly to her and threw me off balance and the frilly dresses and blouses she was always buying me. The clothes were really the worst part now that I was nine and a half and in fourth

2

grade, but still on the chubby side, with short arms and legs. I felt like a fat circus clown when I got dressed up in all those ruffles. I really hated them.

"So," my mom went on, "be good. It's only a few more weeks. Then she'll be well enough to go back to her own apartment."

"A few more weeks." I'd been hearing *that* for weeks. Meantime Grandma Florence was staying in the downstairs den in our house, which was directly under my room. I was supposed to walk quietly up there, couldn't play my records, could hardly even turn over in bed in case the springs squeaked.

"She was more fun," I complained, "when Grandpa Morris was alive."

They were really jolly then, I remembered. Florence-and-Morris, Morris-and-Florence, always together, cracking jokes, telling stories, interrupting one another, fighting, laughing.

"Well, who wouldn't be?" my mom said, jumping up to look at the matzoh balls. "You just don't understand what it's like to be all alone."

"I'm alone," I reminded her. "I'm practically the only kid I know who doesn't have a sister or a brother. I'm an only-only. That's what Grandma Florence always calls me. And I don't mind. In fact, I like it."

3

"Sure you like it. You're the center of attraction. The limelight kid. Bossy as can be. Also you're not sixty-eight years old and having an operation twice a year."

Just then, there it came. "Eh-veh-lyn, Eh-veh-lyn."

"Oh my gosh. Go in to her, Pammy. I can't this minute. These things could suddenly turn to lead and sink to the bottom of the pot."

I crossed the living room to the den. The door was already open. Had she been able to hear us talking?

Grandma Florence was sitting on the edge of the bed and the toilet was still flushing in the connecting bathroom. She smiled wanly.

"Oh," I said, "you're up from your nap."

"Who slept?" she said. "I only rested a little. Come here, darling, and give me a kiss."

She had washed her face and powdered it. When I came close, I could see the powder caked in the deep cracks at the sides of her cheeks. She once told me they were called "laugh lines." But they didn't look so good when you weren't laughing. I kissed her cheek, and of course she grabbed me for a hug.

"Did you finish your homework, sweetie pie? I heard you doing it. Upstairs."

I nodded, deciding not to say anything about the books that had accidentally fallen off my

4

bed and slammed onto the floor.

"So come then," she said, moving carefully back against the pillows and letting out a few sighs of pain over her stitches, which still hurt. "Turn on the set and we'll watch a little television together."

My father said that Grandma Florence always got "the best room in the house" when she came to stay with us, because the big family color television set was in the den.

I walked over to the TV set to turn it on. Then, with my hand on the knob, I hesitated. "Uh-uh," I said, shaking my head, "I just remembered. I'm not allowed."

Grandma Florence looked shocked. "They're punishing you? Why? What for? Tell Grandma what happened."

"Oh no. It's nothing like that. It's on account of school. See, we're having a Turn-Off-the-Tube project. No watching TV for three whole weeks. Until the end of June. We all have to keep a diary telling what we do during the time we would have been sitting in front of the tube."

Grandma Florence was shaking her head. "I never heard of such an idea. Your teacher is some optimist. Doesn't she know television is a fact of life?"

"Ms. Babcock says we don't use our imaginations enough. She says television is a one-way street. Everything gets poured into us and nothing comes out. Anyhow, they're trying it out in lots of schools. It's an experiment."

"And you're the guinea pigs?"

"Yup, I guess. We took a vote on it this afternoon, after we had a long discussion about it. The class is being divided into different groups. Some kids are going to cut down their watching time by one third and some by half. And some are going to watch even less than that."

"But you're not going to watch at all? You're going to cut it out just like that? Cold turkey?"

My mother was standing in the doorway, drying her hands on a towel.

"Evelyn, did you hear? What a daughter you have. She's giving up TV for the duration."

I tried to signal to my mother by making a face but she didn't get my message.

She looked surprised. "It's the first I heard of it. How come you didn't tell me, Pammy?"

"I was going to," I mumbled. "I'm only just starting my project for Ms. Babcock."

That wasn't exactly true. But I'd just that minute decided that it *would* be, starting on Monday.

When Ms. Babcock had asked for volunteers, in school that afternoon, to form a group that wouldn't watch TV at all during the experiment, nobody raised a hand. Now it seemed like a perfect idea. Sure I'd miss a few programs I liked a lot. But I was missing most of them anyway on account of having to watch the programs Grandma Florence liked.

"You really want to keep an eye on that child, Evelyn," Grandma Florence warned. "She always has to lead the parade."

"She's really something," my mother agreed.

They were talking about me as if I wasn't there. But I didn't care. Too bad it was only Friday. I couldn't wait to deliver my blockbuster announcement to the kids in my class. Maybe I'd even make the headlines in the school-district newspaper. I could just see myself, standing on top of a turned-off television set, one fist raised—POW!—in the air, and underneath my picture in big letters: PAMELA TEITELBAUM, FABULOUS FOURTH GRADER, TURNS OFF THE TUBE—COLD TURKEY!

2 Everybody in the classroom was screaming at once.

"No TV *at all?* I'll never believe it!"

"Leave it to her, she always has to be the big
shot."

"How will we know if she's honest?"

I tossed my head back and answered without
turning around. "How will we know if *anybody's* honest? Somebody could watch TV four
hours a day and say they only watched one
hour."

Ms. Babcock clapped for order. "All right.
Enough of this free-for-all. Everybody's on
their honor in this experiment. That goes without saying. Now the important thing is not simply *not* watching TV, but doing constructive
and stimulating things with the time you'll have
instead. Can anybody think of some ideas?"

A few hands shot up and David Traxton
called out, "Cut out paper dolls."

He was the class comic, or so *he* thought, so
nobody paid any attention to that.

Neil Drubnik, who was probably even

dopier, got up from his seat, bowed, and said, "Twiddle your thumbs. Wiggle your ears."

Everybody booed, and Ms. Babcock tossed back her limp blond hair and said, "Now that we've heard from the comedians, who have no doubt been watching too much TV, how about some serious suggestions?"

"I have one," Sharon Marple said shyly. She was probably the most serious person in the whole class. "You could take care of your baby sister."

There were lots of low groans.

"Or your baby brother," Sharon added, before sitting down in embarrassment. Sharon had both in her family. In fact, she was the oldest of six kids.

"Yes, helping around the house," Ms. Babcock agreed. "Some others?"

"Grow a vegetable garden," somebody called out.

"Go to the library more," said somebody else.

"Learn to ride a unicycle."

"Open a lemonade stand on a hot street corner."

"Build a birdhouse."

"Learn the Morse code."

"Take up worm farming."

There were a few "ughs" and screeches.

9

"Good, good," Ms. Babcock said. "Sharon has at least gotten us started thinking constructively."

Philip Barber said, "If Pamela isn't going to watch TV at all for the next three weeks, what's *she* going to do with all her extra time?"

Leave it to Phil. He was always trying to get to me. And when I turned around to look at him, he had that smirky expression on his face.

Ms. Babcock looked at me inquiringly. In fact, the whole class seemed to be waiting. Maybe they thought of me as pretty far out right now, but they were sure paying attention.

I stood up and faced the class. "I have plans," I said, in a soft, husky voice, "but I can't talk about them now. It's a very big and important project, though." Then I sat down.

At afternoon break, Phil sidled up to me. "What a fake you are," he said. "You're such a windbag."

"Oh yeah," I said, making a fist. "Well, if I am, just remember it takes one to know one." Phil Barber couldn't fool me. He did plenty of sneaky things. I'd once caught him copying spelling words for a test that were written on a Band-Aid he'd taken out of his pocket and wrapped around his finger.

"Think you're pretty smart, huh?" he said, slinking away.

I didn't even bother to answer him. Of course I had plans for what I was going to do with my extra time from not watching television. I just didn't happen to know what they were—yet.

A couple of days later, after finishing all the books I had around the house, I went to the library to return them and get some others. I selected an armful of new books from the shelf and sat down at one of the big wooden tables in the children's section to look them over.

Sitting directly across from me, behind a big pile of newspapers and magazines that belonged to the library and were stamped REFERENCE in red ink, was this very suspicious-looking person.

At first, I tried hard not to stare or pay any attention to her. But I just couldn't help myself. Part of the reason was that there was this very strange sound, the faintest little noise, coming from just underneath the table. It went *squeak* and then it went *snip-snip*. Squeak . . . snip-snip; squeak . . . snip-snip.

After a while, I got up to put back some of the books I didn't want, and sneaked around behind her. Sure enough, this person was cutting something out of a magazine that she was carefully holding in her lap.

I glanced down at the floor, beside her chair.

11

There was an old canvas shopping bag and it was overflowing with grocery coupons, the kind that showed you could get ten cents off if you bought a carton of Smooth Smear margarine, twenty-five cents discount on Happy Cat cat food—things like that. And then I saw that she also had a whole bunch of already cut-out coupons on her lap, peeking out from under the magazine.

I continued on over to the library shelves, still trying to mind my own business like everyone was always telling me I was supposed to. By the time I got back to the table, she had finished with the magazine and she had a big newspaper raised up in front of her. I sat down and there was that sound again. Squeak . . . snip-snip; squeak . . . snip-snip.

This was really too much.

I scrambled up onto my library chair on my knees, planted my elbows on the table, and leaned across it as far as I could.

"Listen," I whispered in a deep, hoarse voice, "you're *not* supposed to be doing that."

Down came the newspaper. And there was the face of this little old woman with the strangest eyes I'd ever seen. They were a pale yellow-green and looked just like polished glass from a bottle of lemon-lime soda.

"Sez who?" said the old woman. She had

sharp, broken, little white teeth, and tiny pucker lines all around her mouth.

"Sez me," I replied, ". . . uh . . . I." You could see she was tough. But, after all, I was right. "These magazines and newspapers in the library are for everybody to read," I told her. "You're not supposed to cut them up."

She just stared back at me with those eyes.

"Listen, Pieface, why don't you mind yer own business? I got my business. You got yours. Mind it."

Hmmmph. I backed down a little. Boy, she was someone I'd have liked to have sicced on Philip Barber.

I wriggled more toward my side of the table. "What do you mean, 'business'?"

"I mean what I sez. Business."

"You mean business-business, like something you make money from?"

She folded up the newspaper and started to unfold another. "That's what I mean all right. You sure are a nosy little kid, aren't you?"

"No," I said, settling back into my chair and trying to act a little more friendly. "I'm just interested. My mother cuts those coupons out of the newspaper sometimes, but only the ones she can use. Like, what would be the use of a coupon for cat food if we haven't got a cat, or for frozen fish sticks if I just hate fish? But you're

13

cutting out all of them, every single one that's there."

"Got my reasons," she mumbled. "Got my reasons." She had started snipping again with what had turned out to be a pair of teeny-tiny scissors. Squeak . . . snip-snip.

She didn't seem too mad or fierce now, so I got off my chair and walked around to hers. She was carefully cutting around the dotted lines of a coupon that said forty cents off on a pound of Java Mountain coffee.

"You'd have to buy a whole can of coffee to get forty cents off," I remarked. "And all different kinds of groceries and things to be able to use all those coupons. It'd cost you a bundle. You must have an enormous family."

She just went right on cutting, transferring the coupons from her lap to her shopping bag as they piled up.

"Don't have no family. Not a smidge. I'm an independent operator, dearie. All on my own."

I looked down at the big, crumpled cloth bag at her feet. Something clicked in my head.

"You a bag lady?"

She stopped snipping instantly and glared at me, her lips tightly drawn back from her teeth.

"What'd you just say, miss?"

"A bag lady," I repeated, getting a little scared again. We didn't have any I knew of in our town, which was on the South Shore of Long Island. But I'd seen a few in the city, in certain parts of Manhattan, which was where Grandma Florence lived. They usually sat in doorways or against the sides of buildings, dressed in old clothes and surrounded by bulging plastic or burlap bags filled with all their belongings and with other things they'd picked up out of trash cans and dumps. My mother said they were lonely people who'd had sad and terrible lives and wanted to prove they could get along without anybody's help.

She shook her finger at me. "Now, see here, sister, I am no such thing and don't you ever, ever call me that. I got a name and an address. Got my own little place. Not fancy, but four walls. Pay my rent. Also got lots of important business to attend to. Now, today's my day at the library. Always come to the library on Wednesdays to do my clippin'. And you're interferin', if you must know."

"Sorry," I mumbled. "I was only wondering. And it's still not right to be spoiling magazines for other people who might want to read them." I glanced around, but actually there wasn't anybody in sight just then.

"Aw, quit preachin' at me," she said disgustedly. She waggled a page of a magazine at me. "This stuff's just ads, junk, nothin'. It's not fit readin' for anybody. But for me it's got its uses. Got to think about myself, ya know. Nobody else does."

She was beating me down fast. "Just one more question," I said. "How come you're sitting way over here in the children's section? Most grown-ups sit over there." I pointed across the room to where a lot of older people usually gathered in the afternoons, leafing through magazines and looking lonely.

She let out a sigh of impatience. "You're a smart kid. Figure it out for yourself, Pieface."

I walked back to my side of the table. "My name's not Pieface," I said quietly. "It's Pamela. Pamela Ann Teitelbaum."

I gathered up the books that I was going to check out. "And I have to go home now," I announced, "because it's almost time for supper."

She glanced up at the ceiling. "Well, thanks be for that. I'll be glad to see the back of you." She whipped out a new magazine to start cutting up. Then, surprisingly, she held out her hand. "Oh, by the way, my name's Shirley Brummage. You can call me Shirley. But, remember, don't you *never* call me a bag lady."

I grinned. "See ya around, Shirley."

We shook hands and she looked me straight in the eye.

"I sure hope not, Pieface."

16

3 I walked home from school with Cindy Post. She was in my class but we weren't exactly friends.

"I'll bet you're jumping out of your tree," she said. "Three whole days of not watching *any* television. I'm allowed to watch only an hour and a half a day and I'm really having withdrawal pains. What do you do instead of watching?"

I shrugged. "Oh, stuff. All kinds of things."

"I'll bet you read a lot."

"Sure."

Cindy shifted her books. "Can't you be more specific? See, I don't know what to write in my logbook. What are you putting in yours?"

I kept on walking, looking straight ahead of me. "I write down whatever I do."

Cindy grabbed my arm. "Pamela, are you *really* not watching at all?"

I wriggled free. "Oh, you too, huh? I guess you've been talking to Phil Barber."

"Have not," she said sulkily. "I just thought maybe you'd help me. But you're just as stuck-

17

up and show-offy as everybody says you are. You never want to share anything."

"Oh," I said indignantly, "that's not true. You want to know what I did yesterday from four o'clock to five o'clock? I went to the library. Took out nine books. And after supper I started reading them."

"What? All nine?"

"No, silly. Just one at a time."

Cindy turned away disappointedly. "I can't read that much. It makes my eyes hurt. And also it makes my jaws hurt. Because as soon as I look at a lot of print I start yawning. Yawn-yawn-yawn. Once I start I can't stop until I close the book."

"Well," I said stubbornly, "you asked me and I told you. So don't say I don't share things."

"Maybe you do and maybe you don't," Cindy said teasingly. "In class you said something about an 'important project.' Why did you have to act so mysterious? Lots of other people gave out suggestions."

"Why don't you use one of theirs?" I offered, trying to be helpful.

"Yeah," she said sourly. " 'Learn the Morse code.' 'Start a worm farm.' Honestly!"

"Don't blame me," I said. "I'm doing the best I can. I have my own problems."

And I did. Grandma Florence had a whole new idea when I got home that afternoon. She was propped up on a lot of pillows on the living-room couch and talking to my mother.

"I feel so sorry for the poor child, Evelyn. She's walking around like a lost sheep. I decided it isn't fair that I should watch television and she shouldn't. So I'm giving it up, too."

I could hear all this from the kitchen where I was gulping a glass of milk and smearing peanut butter and jelly on crackers.

"Darling," Grandma Florence said when I walked into the living room. "As soon as you finish your homework, come down to me. We'll play cards. I'll teach you pinochle, canasta, gin rummy, whatever you like. We'll have a lot of fun."

She turned to my mother. "You know, Evelyn, I didn't play cards since Morris died. It's nearly two years already. I think it's time I got back into the mainstream of life."

Grandma Florence winked at me. "So, what do you say, honey bunch?"

I looked at my mother. I could tell from her expression that she was trying to get me to say yes. Now that Grandma Florence was feeling better, she wasn't having an afternoon nap anymore and she wanted company all the time.

19

"Well," I said hesitantly, "I don't know about today. I have an awful lot of homework. It could take me until suppertime."

"All right," Grandma Florence said agreeably. "But maybe you'll finish sooner than you think. If not, we'll play after supper."

After about an hour my mother came upstairs and tapped on the door of my room. I snapped shut the library book I was reading and threw some papers with math examples on them around onto the floor.

"Pammy," she said, looking down at the still-settling papers, "do you really have so much homework?"

"Ummm. Yes."

She picked up the book I'd been reading and flipped through it.

"Ummm. No," she said. "Am I right?"

"Why can't I read a library book if I want to?" I squeaked, trying to keep my voice down.

"Because, Pammy," she said, with a heavy sigh, "I need you. I need you to help take the load off me. Why can't you go down to Grandma and play cards with her a little? It's only a few more . . ."

"Weeks!" I filled in.

"No. Less. Really. She's getting better quickly now."

"Then why can't she go home?" We were

both whispering hotly and heavily now.

My mother rubbed the back of her hand across her forehead.

"Because she's not *that* much better. She's just in between. I have her all day long Monday to Friday. She wants to talk, talk, talk. I can't even get the beds made. Or the cooking done. She has no friends around here, and it's too far away for her friends to come and visit her. And now she has this crazy idea that she won't watch television. Not even in the mornings. It's all because of you, Pammy. What a time you picked. As if I don't know the real reason."

I looked at her through screwed-up eyes. "What do you mean, the 'real reason'?"

"Pammy, just remember, I'm very tuned in to you. You might fool your father and even your Grandma, but not me. I know you're trying to avoid spending time with her. But I expect you to share some of the duties around here. Starting right now."

That's what I meant about my mother being so moody lately. She'd be fine one minute and start getting really bossy the next.

I picked up the book I'd been reading. "I'll play cards with her after supper."

"No," she said angrily. "Your father will be home then, and he can take over. I want you down there *now!*"

"Okay, okay," I whispered. "You don't have to get hysterical about it."

"They're delicious, delicious," Grandma Florence was saying as she sampled something from a platter. "A little more pepper and a little less salt and you'd have them almost perfect, Evelyn."

My father had come home and we were having supper. Grandma Florence was feeling well enough to come to the table instead of having a tray in the den. Everyone was feeling pretty happy tonight.

Grandma Florence said it was a special occasion because just before supper my grown-up cousin Lainie had phoned. She and her boyfriend had just "named the date." They were getting married late in the summer.

"A small wedding," Grandma Florence was explaining. "Very simple. In good taste, you know what I mean?"

My father nodded, his glasses glinting, and laughed. "Where've I heard that song before? They all start out small."

"Wait a minute," I said. "How small? Lainie promised me I'd be her flower girl when she got married to Elliot. She said I'd scatter white rose petals at her feet. White rose petals. That job belongs to me."

22

"Of course, of course," my father said, as he plopped mashed potatoes onto his plate.

"Let's not worry about that now," my mother said, as she jabbed a fork into something round and fried-looking from the platter and dropped it onto my plate.

"What's this?" I looked down at it and wrinkled my nose. "Smells funny."

"Try it," Grandma Florence said. "One of my recipes I finally got your mother to prepare." She looked up at my mother and nodded. "They didn't come out bad, Evelyn. Could use a little lemon juice. And pepper. White, not black."

I looked around the table. There was beginning to be a funny silence. Only Grandma Florence still acted happy and normal.

I began to cut into the fried thing on my plate. "What do you mean, 'Let's not worry about it'? Aren't they having a flower girl at the wedding?" I asked my mother. "Did they pick somebody else? I have to know about it."

"Why?" my father asked. "Is it so important?"

"Sure it's important. I told you it's a promise Lainie made to me. We even talked about the dress I would wear and the wreath for my hair—"

"Pamela," my mother interrupted, "you'll be

23

a flower girl some other time."

I jammed the piece of fried thing into my mouth. "What do you mean, 'some other time'? I'll be too old. I won't be small and . . . oh, *yuk*, how *disgusting!*"

I had just swallowed something awful-tasting. It was too late to spit it out. I gagged and began to choke. "Fish!" I howled. "On top of everything else you give me fish for supper. You know I hate it!"

There was a terribly loud crash from my father's end of the table. A water glass jumped and droplets flew up into the air. He looked down at his fist and slowly began to unclench it.

"Sidney, control yourself," Grandma Florence said in alarm. "So the child hates fish. I thought my recipe for salmon croquettes she'd like. Don't blame her. Blame me."

My father didn't say a word. But I thought I saw a smile just flickering at the corner of my mother's mouth. Maybe I was wrong.

Then Grandma Florence turned to me. "I'm sorry, darling. Fish is brain food, so I only thought . . . But you've got enough brains as it is. And about the wedding, I'm just thinking. Lainie is my oldest granddaughter and you're my youngest. Why shouldn't both be in the ceremony?"

She looked around the table. My father was

still red-faced. My mother's eyes were fixed on her plate.

"Leave it to Grandma, darling. I'll fix it. I'll call Lainie back and I'll talk to her. It will be arranged."

Nobody said a word.

Grandma Florence went on blithely. "And then, after supper," she said, looking pointedly at my silent parents, "Mommy and Daddy will go to the movies for a little relaxation. And you and I, Pamela . . . we'll play a little cards."

4 I could just imagine what my logbook for Ms. Babcock was going to look like:

Thursday 3:30 to 4:30   Did homework
           4:30 to 6:00   Played cards with
                                   Grandma Florence
           6:00 to 7:00   Ate supper
           7:00 to bedtime Played cards with
                                   Grandma Florence

Was that my big project, the creative and constructive thing that I was going to do for three weeks while not watching television? It was nearly as ordinary as Sharon Marple's suggestion to take care of the little kids in her family. After all my boasting I had to think of something unusual . . . and *fast*. But what?

Today in class, Cindy Post had been staring at me oddly and so had a lot of the other kids. Or was it my imagination? So I was glad to have a good excuse to escape early, after the dismissal bell rang. My mother had asked me to stop at the candy store and pick up some magazines for

Grandma Florence. She wrote the names down on a list. "Especially, Pammy, be sure to get her *Reader's Digest*. That's the one she reads the most carefully. It should keep her busy for a couple of hours anyway."

While I was waiting impatiently for my change, I leafed through a couple of the magazines I was buying. A page fell open to a cardboard-like sheet of advertising with a ten-cents-off coupon for instant pistachio pudding. I flipped the page. There was a coupon for baby talcum. The next page had one for frozen pizza. Nearly every page had something.

I rushed home thinking about the coupons. Grandma Florence would probably finish the magazines in a couple of days. Then she'd surely let me cut out the coupons. But what of it? I didn't know what to do with them. Only Shirley Brummage did. I had to find her.

But the moment I burst in the front door, I forgot all about Shirley Brummage. From Grandma Florence's den came the sound of high-pitched laughing. Too giggly for my mother or Grandma Florence. Somebody was visiting. I rushed into the room with my schoolbooks and the magazines.

"Lainie!" I was both thrilled and a little embarrassed at seeing her. Had Grandma Florence called her here because I'd nearly had a fit last night at the dinner table about not being a flower girl at her wedding?

Lainie swung her head of shining pale brown hair in a happy greeting. "Hey, look who's here."

I ran over and hugged her. Her cheeks were flushed and she was sparkling-eyed, prettier than ever. It was always hard for me to remember that Lainie was a reading teacher. And that Elliot, whom she was going to marry, was a psychologist. The teacher who taught the kids with special reading problems in our school didn't look a bit like Lainie.

"And no kiss for Grandma Florence?" came a voice from the bed where Grandma Florence was sitting up against the pillows.

I went over obediently, kissed her cheek, and handed her all the magazines at once. Grandma Florence didn't look very sick anymore, but maybe she wanted Lainie to think she was. A little, anyway.

"I'll have you know," Lainie said, looking straight at Grandma Florence, "that I was *summoned* here this afternoon. I had to rush away from school early because your grandma said we had to discuss some very important things about my forthcoming . . . ahem . . . nuptials."

My mother, who had been sitting on a has-

sock near the TV all this time, jumped up. "I'll
make some coffee."

Lainie grabbed her arm. "No, don't, Aunt
Evvie. Really." She glanced at her watch. "I've
got to go. I'm leaving this minute."

"You're going?" I said, disappointed. I
looked from her to Grandma Florence. "I
thought you two had to . . . talk."

"We did already," Lainie said. "It isn't en-
tirely up to me, though. You understand,
Pamela, I have to discuss it with Elliot and with
my folks and his folks."

"Sure," Grandma Florence agreed. "Discuss
it, Lainie. Discuss it all you like."

"We had a very simple ceremony in mind,"
Lainie went on almost apologetically. "People
just aren't going in for an army of attendants
these days."

What did she mean? I wondered. Had she
changed her mind about me?

"One flower girl isn't what I would call an
'army of attendants,'" Grandma Florence remarked.

"I know, Grandma," Lainie said, "but these
things have a way of mushrooming. Still"—she
looked at me lovingly—"I know I did once
make Pamela a promise. I'll just have to see
what I can do."

*

29

After Lainie left, Grandma Florence caught my eye and winked at me. I guess she was trying to tell me not to worry too much about the outcome. Then she heaved a sigh and turned contentedly to her magazines.

I dashed upstairs and did part of my homework. But I kept wondering how I was going to get in touch with Shirley Brummage about all those coupons I was going to have for her. So, after a while, I went downstairs to look her up in the telephone book.

After nearly tripping over me twice in the front hall, where I was down on all fours poring over the directory, my mother insisted on knowing what I was looking up.

"Oh, the phone number of somebody in my class," I answered. "But I'm not sure how she spells her name."

I had already tried Brummage, Brummich, Brummidge, and Brummitch, both with one *m* and two *m*'s. But there was no such name.

"Really," my mother said, "can't you wait until you see her in school?"

"That's just it," I replied. "I won't. I mean—I can't. No, I can't wait because it's part of my homework assignment. I think I'll have to go to the library instead." I scrambled to my feet and shoved the phone directory into the drawer. "Yup, that's what I'll do."

A few minutes later, I was out the door. I didn't really expect to find Shirley Brummage in the library. She had said Wednesdays were her day for doing her clippings. But maybe someone there could tell me where she lived.

I hung around near the main desk until the librarian with the kindest-looking face wasn't busy. It wasn't easy describing Shirley Brummage. How could I ask for the old woman with the shopping bag who cut coupons out of all the reference magazines and newspapers on the sly?

"I really don't know who you mean," the librarian said. "But wait a minute. I'll ask somebody who might know."

A large freckle-faced woman with short reddish blond hair and a deep, booming voice came out of the office behind the desk.

"Is it your grandmother you're looking for, dear?"

I shook my head. "Uh-uh. She's no relation."

"Oh, I see. A neighbor, then." She looked over toward the group of tables where the older people usually gathered in the afternoons.

"And she isn't here now?" she inquired sympathetically.

I didn't understand that question at all. If she were here, why would I be asking for her at the desk?

31

"No." She answered her own question. "You've looked and she isn't here. Is she one of our regulars, do you know?"

"She usually comes to the library on Wednesdays," I told her, "and she sits in the children's section. She doesn't like to sit around and gab with the others. She's a . . ." I tried to think of the words Shirley had used. "She's a . . . an independent operator."

"Oh, then I wouldn't know. I'm not here on Wednesdays. But I wouldn't panic if I were you. I doubt that she's lost."

"Of course, she isn't lost," I said emphatically. "Just because I'm looking for her and can't find her doesn't mean she's lost."

I left the library feeling really discouraged. I stood on the steps scratching my head. All of a sudden, somebody bopped me hard on the shoulder.

I turned, startled and angry. It was Phil Barber, the last person I wanted to see.

"Listen, you keep your hands to yourself!"

He grinned. "Wasn't my hands." He held up a book. It was large and flat.

"Oh," I said, making a mocking face. "What are you reading now, *Horton Hears a Who* or *Yertle the Turtle*?"

"Very funny," he said. "This happens to be

an excellent book on photography. I'm building my own darkroom in the basement. That's what *I'm* doing with my spare time while I'm watching less television. Cindy Post says you're reading. She says you take out nine books at a time."

"What's wrong with that?"

"Nothing. It's great. Except it's not very original. Not after the way you acted in front of the class. You always have to play the big shot, don't you, Pamela?"

I shrugged. "I can't help it if I get good ideas."

"Yeah," he said. "Well, the day of reckoning is coming. We're all waiting to see your logbook. Then we'll know the truth."

"What truth?" I demanded, beginning to get steaming mad.

"The truth about whether you *really* gave up watching TV at all."

"Are you calling me a liar, Phil Barber?"

He took the library steps in a single leap. "*You* said it. I didn't."

"O-h-h-h," I howled after him, "I hope your whole darkroom . . . blows up!"

I began walking home, kicking everything in sight—empty soda cans, scrunched-up paper containers, bottle caps, ice-cream cups, cigarette wrappers. There was litter and rubbish everywhere, plenty of stuff to kick at.

All of a sudden I came to a little kid's beat-up wagon. It was standing in somebody's driveway, right in the middle of the sidewalk. It, too, was loaded with rubbish—squashed beer cans, bottles, some of them broken, batches of old newspapers. I kicked at the rim of the wagon. What a place to leave it.

"Hey," someone called out sharply. "Keep your feet to yourself. That ain't your property." There was something familiar, tough, and snappy about that voice.

I looked up into the driveway. There, bending over a pile of trash, was Shirley Brummage. She was wearing an old, faded green raincoat and dirty white sneakers. I clapped both hands to my head in disbelief.

"I was looking for you," I called out delightedly. "I was just over at the library asking them if they knew where you lived. And here you are."

"Worse luck," she muttered. She didn't seem the least bit glad to see me.

"Oh, it's okay," I assured her. "They didn't know who you were. They didn't know anything about the coupons you cut out the other day." Her eyes glared at me fiercely. Curled over the trash heap with that puckery mouth and close-cropped gray-white hair, she looked more like a cat than ever. "And don't worry," I added. "I would never tell them what you did . . . Shirley."

She straightened up. "Let's get out of here."

"Why?" I looked up at the two-story brick house alongside the driveway. "Isn't this where you live?"

"Course not, dummy. This is a mansion compared to where I live. I'm just out on one of my antique-huntin' jaunts."

"Can you really find antiques in people's garbage?"

"Not garbage, kiddy. Trash. I don't hunt garbage. What do you think I am?"

She headed for the beat-up kid's wagon and grabbed hold of the handle. So it belonged to her. I might have known.

I glanced down at the rubbish in it. "Well, what's this stuff then?"

"This is recyclables. Don't you know *nothin'*?"

With a sigh of exasperation, she dropped the wagon handle and started counting out on her fingers.

"Look, I'll explain it to yer. There's three things ya gotta know. First, there's trash. That's old or worn-out or broken stuff. Maybe it's antiques, maybe it's just old-time junk, flea-market stuff. Maybe it can be fixed, maybe not. Anyhow, you take that stuff to a dealer by the

35

load. Unless you got a direct sale, of course. That's the first thing. You understand?"

I bobbed my head. "Um hmmm."

"Okay. Now, next you got recyclables like I been collectin' here in the wagon. That's metal, paper, glass. Stuff like that."

"Oh, right," I said, trying to show how quickly I was catching on. "Only what do you do with them?"

"You take 'em to the recyclin' station," she said, looking at me in disbelief. "There's one out the north end of town. They weigh it up and pay you by the pound. Gad, where you been all your life?"

"I'm only nine and a half," I reminded her.

"That's no excuse," she snapped. "You gotta know these things. Where do you think I'd be today if I didn't learn my business from top to bottom? You think somebody comes up to you in the street and tells you these things outa the goodness of their hearts?"

"I guess not. What's the third thing?"

"The third thing's garbage. Rot. Decayin' vegetables, fruit, meat, bones, fat, skin. They can recycle that, too, into fertilizer and the like. But I don't have no truck with it. Two things don't you never call me, Pieface. You don't call me a bag lady and you don't call me a garbage collector."

36

She picked up the handle of the wagon and started down the street.

"Where are we going next?" I asked, trotting along beside her and thinking of the cans I'd kicked along the street, wondering if I should offer to go back and get them.

" 'We'? You thinkin' of cuttin' in on my business? 'Cause if you are, m'dear, you better just unthink it."

"Oh no," I assured her. "I'm just thinking of something useful to do. It's pretty constructive, wouldn't you say, picking up litter off the street and finding good stuff in people's trash, and carting it off to the recycling plant or the junk dealer's. I'd like to help. Honestly."

She looked at me suspiciously. "No cuttin' in on my take?"

"Uh-uh. Never. In fact, one of the reasons I was looking for you, Shirley, was to tell you that I'm going to have a whole bunch of brand-new coupons for you in a couple of days. Do you have some kind of a dealer who pays you money for those, too?"

"I'll take 'em," she said briskly. "Coupons is one of my sidelines. But I can't tell you what I do with 'em, Pieface. See, I'd have to know ya better."

Just then I spotted a couple of flattened soda pop cans lying near the curb, and I scurried over to get them. "Didn't you remember my name?" I called over my shoulder. "It's Pamela."

I came over and tossed the cans into the wagon. She smiled, showing a few sharp little white teeth. "Yeah, I remember. There ain't much I forget, Pieface."

5 I was in the best mood yet, ready to stick my tongue out at the whole world. And especially at Phil Barber.

Maybe Shirley Brummage didn't look the part in her shapeless raincoat, torn sneakers, and thick brown stockings. But she was the closest thing to a fairy godmother. She gave me my "project" for my logbook. And I dared anybody in the whole fourth grade to come up with a better one for the Turn-Off-the-Tube experiment.

Afternoons I'd meet Shirley to go trash hunting and to collect stuff for the recycling plant. You wouldn't believe the kinds of things people threw out—old radios and toasters, table-model phonographs, records, books, toys, old clothes, furniture, dishes. We even found a bigger wagon with only one broken wheel that we started to use for collecting.

Of course, we couldn't handle big things like TV's and refrigerators. But Shirley had an instinct for when somebody was going to clean out their attic or their basement, or move, or get rid of a lot of stuff that didn't sell at last week's garage sale. She said she could "sniff it in the air."

Some days we'd make two or even three trips to different junk dealers to unload and start out fresh. They all knew Shirley, and if they didn't pay her what she thought the stuff was worth she gave them a really hard time. Some of the dealers ran little antique or used-furniture shops and some just had plain old junkyards. One of the biggest and messiest junkyards, I found out, was a place that a lot of artists came to, looking for old pieces of metal and wood to use in making sculpture. They even called them "junk sculptures."

Loading up with recyclables was so easy, it was boring. There was no end to the soda cans and paper containers that people kept throwing in the street, mostly out of car windows. It was a long walk to the recycling station pulling our two wagons, so we tried to leave that for cooler days or times when there just didn't seem to be much worthwhile trash around.

"They ought to pay us extra for cleaning up the streets," I told Shirley one afternoon when I was especially hot and sweaty from picking up heaps of cans and bottles. The weather was getting warmer and people must have been getting thirstier.

"Ha!" she said. "That'd be askin' for egg in yer beer, Pieface."

I didn't understand for sure what she meant by that, but sometimes Shirley got impatient when I asked her to explain things. And she kept right on calling me Pieface. Never once Pamela.

But I had to stay on the good side of her. I still didn't know where she lived or what she did with all those coupons I was clipping for her from Grandma Florence's magazines and anything else I could get my hands on. It was enough that the trash collecting was keeping me away from the TV set just the way Ms. Babcock would have wanted it to.

At home, things were getting better, too. Grandma Florence was actually getting ready to move back to her own apartment. My mother was in better spirits, my father was more talkative, and sure enough—just as Grandma Florence had hinted to me after Lainie's visit—Lainie's wedding was going to be just big enough to have one flower girl and I was going to be it!

On the evening before Grandma Florence left, we had a backyard cookout, the first of the season. We sat around the outdoor table with its checkered plastic tablecloth, and my father made toasts to Grandma Florence's health with grape juice.

Grandma Florence was in a really jolly mood.

"You're not fooling me for one minute," she said to my mother and father. "You're both glad to be getting rid of me. The only one who's going to miss me here is Pamela."

My parents laughed. For the last week or so, I'd been meeting Shirley Brummage almost every day right after I got home from school. And after supper, I'd been cooped up in my room doing my homework.

"Oh, it's all right," Grandma Florence went on with a knowing wink, "that lately Pamela's been neglecting her Grandma a little. She only did it because she knew I was feeling better. After all, the child has a perfect right to go out and play with her friends after school."

My mother gave me a meaningful sidelong glance. It was all too true. Except, of course, nobody in my family knew that my so-called friends were really Shirley Brummage. It had all seemed too complicated to explain, and besides I wanted to keep it a secret from everyone until the day I handed in my Turn-Off-the-Tube report to Ms. Babcock.

We all dug into the steaks that my father had cooked on the grill. Grandma Florence said they were "perfect," and I noticed she didn't say "almost perfect" like she did about my mother's cooking.

When we got to the ice cream and cake, Grandma Florence looked up and said slyly to my mother, "Evelyn, when are you going to tell Pamela your surprise?"

My mother was serving the ice cream and she stopped, holding the ice-cream scoop in midair.

"Oh," was all she said.

I could tell Grandma Florence's remark was unexpected and that my mother was confused. Some ice cream dripped off the scoop and ran down her arm. She dabbed at it quickly.

"It's a little early," my mother mumbled. "I wasn't going to say anything just yet."

My father grabbed the empty scoop from my mother and served himself a big dollop of peach ice cream. He didn't seem as happy as he'd been a little while ago.

"I did it again, didn't I?" Grandma Florence said with an air of helplessness. "I opened my mouth and I put my foot in it, huh?"

"You certainly did, Mom," my father agreed.

My mother didn't say anything, but she looked embarrassed.

"What's the surprise?" I asked. I was already getting the feeling that it wasn't going to be such a good one. "They aren't calling off the wedding or something like that, are they?"

"Oh no," my mother reassured me. "That wouldn't be a surprise, would it, Pammy? That would be a disappointment. Right?"

There was something a little too sweet and babying about the way my mother was talking to me. I didn't like this at all.

"You'd better tell me," I said. "It's not fair saying there's a surprise and then not telling what it is."

"She's right, Evelyn. Now that the cat is out of the bag, what good is it beating around the bush?" That was Grandma Florence, of course, only making me even more anxious and worried about what was going on.

My mother grabbed the ice-cream scoop from my father and dug it fiercely into the open ice-cream container on the table.

"Ma," she said, not looking at Grandma Florence at all, "you really don't know when to quit, do you?"

It was the first time I'd heard my mother sound so angry at Grandma Florence. She dug out a few more balls of ice cream, flung them into a bowl, shut the container, and disappeared into the house.

Grandma Florence turned worriedly to my father. "What did I do, Sidney? What did I do? Was it so terrible to mention you're expecting a . . . a new visitor? The child has to know sooner or later. Better sooner. She'll have more time to get used to the idea."

I was getting the idea very quickly now, and I didn't plan on ever getting used to it. For nine and a half years I'd been the only child in the family and I was used to *that*. I knew all about baby sisters and brothers, and I needed a new kid in the house about as much as Sharon Marple did. How could my parents do a mean, sneaky thing like this to me? I was furious.

"All right, all right," Grandma Florence was saying to my father. "A person has to watch every word they say around here. I see I overstayed my welcome. In which case, I refuse to spend another night in this house. I'll go inside this minute and pack, and you can drive me home tonight, Sidney. Or better yet, you can call me a cab!"

My father pushed away his uneaten dessert. I could see his face getting red and his fist getting ready to slam down on the table. With a screech, I leaped from my seat and raced toward the house.

"Oh, for crying out loud!" my father roared. "Pamela, get back here," he called after me.

"No," I yelled hoarsely. "You just ruined my entire life. I hate you. Mom, too. Both of you!"

6 At the back door, I slammed headlong into my mother, who was just coming out of the house. And the first thing I did was to make a fist and punch her hard in the belly.

"Pamela!"

She grabbed my wrists and dragged me screaming into the kitchen.

"Cut it out," she gasped. "Cut it out this minute. What's come over you?"

I kept right on fighting her. And every time I got one of my wrists free, I punched her wherever I could—pow, POW, P-O-W.

I wrestled with her the way I would have with one of the kids from school, the way I'd have liked to have socked Phil Barber when he got me mad, worse . . . the way I'd want to sock my best friend if she did something really ratty to me.

All of a sudden I felt my bottom bounced down hard on a kitchen chair. And, just like that, all the fight seemed to drain right out of me. A tear plopped onto my knee. I hadn't even known I was crying.

My mother was leaning back against the kitchen sink and studying me, one hand to her cheek and her elbow resting in her other hand. She was still breathing hard, but her expression was calm and I noticed she'd put on some pale pink lipstick while she was in the house.

When she saw how quiet and sorry I was, she came over and knelt down beside my chair. She began wiping my cheeks and my eyes with a hankie. And the next thing I did was to put my arms around her and really cry.

We just rocked back and forth like that for a while. I couldn't tell if she was crying or not, because I was getting my own wet, sticky tears all over her.

When we finally separated our heads, her hair was all messed up and her lipstick was smeary.

"Did I hurt you?" I croaked, thinking of the way I'd punched her in the stomach.

She looked at me sadly and shook her head.

"I didn't . . . kill anything, did I?"

My mother frowned.

"What's wrong, Pammy? You're talking strangely."

"You know. *It* . . . whatever it is. Oh, I don't want it. Really, I don't. But I still didn't mean to hurt you. . . ."

"Pammy." She was still on her knees next to

47

my chair and she shook me gently by the shoulders. "There's some misunder . . . oh, oh, oh!" She began to laugh. "I think I know now what you've been thinking." She shook her head in disbelief. "You thought that was the surprise your grandmother was talking about, didn't you? You thought I was going to have a baby."

"You aren't?" I asked.

She shook her head, smiling.

"You honestly aren't? Cross your heart?"

"I honestly 'aren't.' Now see what you get for jumping to conclusions. Oh, really, Pammy, when will you learn not to be such a hothead?"

I slapped my hand to my forehead, remembering the scene in the backyard. "And Grandma and Daddy had a big fight over it, too. She wants to go home tonight. In a taxi."

My mother jumped to her feet in dismay. "Oh no! What a mess. This whole thing has gotten blown up out of proportion. I was going to tell you, Pammy. I just thought I'd wait until things were calmer, until after Grandma Florence left."

"But why?" I urged. "Is it something you're afraid to tell me? Something bad?"

My mother folded her arms and leaned back against the sink.

"No, not at all. It's something good."

I hunched forward anxiously.

"The surprise, Pammy, is that we're going to have someone staying with us this summer."

I instantly collapsed.

"What! So soon after Grandma Florence is leaving?"

I could just picture some other version of Grandma Florence moving into the den, me having to tiptoe around in my room, everybody tied up in knots all over again. "Are you *nuts?*"

"Sssh," my mother commanded. "And don't use that word to me, Pam. This is something very different. This is somebody for *you.* She's a little older but not much, eleven and a half, and I know you're going to be very good friends, sisters even. There's a long summer ahead, and it can really be a time of sharing and learning and growing together."

I couldn't believe what my mother was saying. This was even worse than having a helpless, brand-new baby around the house. This person was older than I was and probably stuck-up and bossy as well.

"Who is this kid, anyway?" I demanded.

"She's my cousin Sandra's child. You've probably heard me speak of her, though I haven't seen her myself since she was a baby. Since before you were born. She's an only child. Like you."

My mother began to rearrange a glass of flowers on the countertop. "There are some . . . well, problems at home that we won't go into now. She'll be flying East by herself in a couple of weeks, when school's finished. All the way from California. She'll sleep in the upstairs guest room, next to your room, and I want you to make her feel welcome. And wanted. That's important, Pammy. Remember."

I stared down at the linoleum, my hands dangling between my knees. "What's her name?" I asked dejectedly.

"Daphne."

"Can I call her Daffy?"

"No. Not unless she says you can. Meantime, her name is Daff-nee. It's got a *ph* in it that's pronounced 'fuh.' Like in Phyllis."

"Like in Philip," I added glumly. "But Daphne. Really! *I* never heard of it."

In the den, across the living room, drawers were being pulled open and banged shut, and my father and Grandma Florence were mumbling short, angry remarks at one another.

"Now I've got to go in *there* and straighten *that* out," my mother announced grimly.

I really felt sorry for her. I felt sorry for the rotten way I was acting. I wished I could be nicer to her, but how could I? Just look what she was doing to me!

*

It was the last week of school, and my log-book was fourteen pages thick. It was crammed full of details about my Turn-Off-the-Tube project, about the afternoons of cleanups and trash collecting that I'd spent with Shirley Brummage, and the evenings of doing my homework and reading the books I'd taken out of the library. I hadn't watched TV once, hadn't even peeked, and that was the honest truth.

The day after Ms. Babcock collected the reports, we had a discussion about how the kids in the class had felt about the experiment.

"Be honest," Ms. Babcock urged. "If you hated not seeing all your programs, were bored silly trying to think of other things to do, cheated a little because you just couldn't stay away from the tube, let us know."

A few hands went up timidly.

"I really tried," said Lorie Bixby earnestly. "But it was awfully hard. I don't think I could have kept it up another day. But I never cheated by watching any more hours than I was allowed. And one good thing, I lost a little weight."

"Please explain, Lorie."

"Well, because I always eat when I'm watching."

There were a few guffaws from the boys. Lorie *was* sort of plump.

51

"A good reason for cutting down. It could be a double bonus."

Neil Drubnik was waggling his arm.

"Yes, Neil?"

"I cheated, I cheated."

There was a lot of embarrassed laughter.

"Why?"

" 'Cause I like TV. 'Cause it's great. It helps me when I get restless. And you can learn things, too."

"I watched less and I watched better programs," someone said soberly.

There was halfhearted applause.

"I didn't mind missing my programs," somebody called out, "because I'm gonna watch the summer reruns."

"That wasn't exactly the point of the experiment," Ms. Babcock commented. "It was hoped that some new patterns would be established. Does anybody think they'll watch less TV this summer because of the experiment?"

"Yeah," said David Traxton. "I won't watch at all—when I'm at the beach!"

Ms. Babcock pressed her lips together and shook her head. "Let's have a few serious answers. Cindy?"

"I really tried to think of other things to do like you said. But nothing seemed to work. I got so nervous over it that I had to watch TV to relax. But then I felt guilty. So I didn't really enjoy it much." Cindy sat down with a puzzled frown on her face.

"A good thought," said Ms. Babcock. "Hold on to that. It might be the beginning of something."

Ms. Babcock walked around behind her desk. "Now for your logbooks. I want to say a few words about the best ones that were turned in. A few of you showed real creativity and set some very good examples." She looked around the room. "Nobody started a worm farm. How come?"

There were screeches and giggles from the girls and a disgusting sound from Neil Drubnik.

Ms. Babcock lifted up the stack of reports on her desk. "Most of your logs were very carefully worked on, I must say. Although I honestly don't see how it could take twenty minutes to take out the garbage. Or an hour to eat an after-school snack."

"The bag must have broken."

"They ate a twelve-pound turkey."

Ms. Babcock ignored those dumb cracks and so did I. My eyes were glued to the logbooks. At the very top of the pile was mine. I could tell by the thickness and also by the decorated yellow cover I'd made out of heavy paper. On it I had drawn a great big TV set with a blank screen and, in front of it, an empty chair. I thought that said a lot.

"I'm going to talk only about those of you who were really inventive in finding new activities, not just time fillers."

I watched Ms. Babcock intently as she began fingering the pages of my report. "I think the one that is the most outstanding"—she lifted my report and placed it on her desk; then she set the rest of the pile down beside it—"and shows real planning and care, as well as being a highly constructive and rewarding undertaking . . ."

What was Ms. Babcock doing? She was lifting the next report from the top of the pile, probably forgetting that she had already separated mine from the others. I tried hissing softly and pointing my finger at her to get her attention.

But too late. She had already picked up the next report. It was thinner than mine—couldn't she tell that?—and it had a black cover with white letters cut out and pasted onto it.

". . . is this one handed in by . . ."

"No, no," I stage-whispered. "That isn't mine."

Ms. Babcock looked down at me with an odd expression. Then she held up the other report. ". . . is this one handed in by Philip Barber."

7 Philip Barber!
I whacked at my forehead in astonishment and rage, while a bunch of kids in the back of the room whistled and stamped and yelled out, "Yay, Phil!"

Ms. Babcock signaled for quiet.

"Yes, congratulations are due. But let me tell you why I feel Philip turned in the best Turn-Off-the-Tube report in the class."

The "best"! Ms. Babcock was crazy. Phil Barber had only cut his TV watching in half, while I had cut it out altogether. How could you compare building a darkroom with the stuff I'd been doing—cleaning up the streets, taking stuff to the recycling plant, and helping a poor old person earn a living besides? Not that Shirley Brummage ever talked about how poor she was. She didn't have to.

Ms. Babcock went into a lot of gobbledy-gook about how in building his darkroom in the basement Philip Barber was embarking on a hobby with long-range goals and wonderful career possibilities. She went on about how photography would sharpen his mind and his eye and make him more sensitive to the world around him.

And as I listened to all this, getting more and more furious, I remembered that Ms. Babcock almost always came to school with a camera. During the school year she'd taken lots of pictures of our class and she'd even told us how she was an "incurable shutterbug" and a "frustrated professional photographer."

Hmmm. I squinched my eyes together. Phil was tricky. Maybe he cared about photography and maybe he didn't, but he sure knew how to get on the right side of Ms. Babcock.

But there wasn't anything I could say to Ms. Babcock or to any of the kids in the class. They'd only have called me a sore loser.

I turned around to give Phil a look and saw Cindy Post waving her hand frantically.

Finally Ms. Babcock finished praising Phil and called on Cindy.

"Pamela said she wasn't going to watch any TV at all the whole time," Cindy said, in a challenging tone. "We'd like to know what *her* project was." Cindy looked around the room for approval and a lot of people yelled out, "Yeah, yeah. No TV at all."

"Yes," said Ms. Babcock, "I was just coming to that."

She lifted my yellow-covered report off her

desk and held it up in front of the room. There were oohs and aahs about how fat it was. Ms. Babcock flipped the pages.

"I get it, I get it," Neil Drubnik called out. "She copied the telephone book."

There were screams of laughter. Neil Drubnik and David Traxton pounded on their desks. Philip Barber had his mouth wide open in a big guffaw and was wiping his eyes.

"It's not funny!" I exploded, jumping up from the seat and glaring at all their silly laughing faces.

Ms. Babcock looked alarmed for a moment.

"Pamela, would you like to come up here and explain your report to the class?"

"I *am* up here," I fired back. "And yes, I *would.*"

I grabbed my logbook out of her hands and cleared my throat. I had this awful choking sensation, especially when I tried to swallow.

"This report," I began, in a very loud voice, "is about how I spent my time for three whole weeks while I wasn't watching *any television at all. . . .*"

I looked pointedly at Phil Barber and, at that very moment, just as I was getting my breath together for my really big speech, the classroom bell rang for an early dismissal.

Instantly, everybody was out of their seats

57

and the class had turned into a yammering mob.

"I'm sorry, Pamela," Ms. Babcock said, glancing at her watch and taking the logbook out of my hand. "We'll discuss your project tomorrow."

I stared at her accusingly. There was only a day and a half of school left. Tomorrow there was room cleanup in the morning and then the class party in the afternoon. No one would be in the mood to hear about my report.

"I promise you we'll discuss it," she said, probably reading my thoughts. "It's an excellent report."

Tears came to my eyes, but I fought them back by sticking out my lower lip.

"Then why wasn't it best? Why was Phil's best? He copied all that junk out of a book. I saw it. The book, I mean. You're not fair! You just like photography better than junk collecting."

"Pamela, I can't let you say that. I weighed the two reports very carefully. Phil was an avid TV watcher, like most of the others in the class. I thought that showing how *he* found a new interest might serve as a model for them."

"But I turned off the TV altogether," I protested. "And I really knocked myself out picking up all that rubbish and going to the recycling station a couple of times a week. Doesn't anybody *care* about that?"

I reached past Ms. Babcock and snatched my beautiful yellow-covered logbook off her desk.

She looked puzzled.

"What are you doing, Pamela?"

"I'm taking my report. It belongs to *me!*"

The classroom had emptied out. I gathered up the rest of my things and marched toward the open doorway that led into the corridor. Ms. Babcock didn't even try to stop me.

"Please," she called after me in a gentle, worried voice, "please bring it in with you tomorrow, Pamela. We'll discuss it first thing in the morning. You have my solemn promise."

I kept right on going and made believe I didn't even hear her.

School was over for the summer and I was glad. I was still angry at Ms. Babcock, although it didn't matter anymore. She wasn't going to be my teacher in fifth grade and I'd probably hardly ever see her again.

Of course, I hadn't brought my logbook to school with me the next day. Ms. Babcock did keep her promise, though, and she described my project to the class first thing in the morning. But it wasn't at all the way I had planned for it to be. I was only *second* best and all the real praise had gone to Phil Barber the day before.

When Ms. Babcock finished talking about my report, she asked me if there was anything I wanted to add. But I just stayed in my seat and shook my head.

The kids in the class seemed in a quiet mood. They agreed it was a pretty good project, but they didn't yell or stamp the way they had for Phil. At the very end, Sharon Marple raised her hand and said, "That's something we could *all* do this summer. I'd like to make a little extra money."

"I didn't do it for the money," I croaked grumpily from my seat. Ms. Babcock agreed and was quick to point out that my project had been "a noble effort" in two ways, first because I was "performing a public service," and secondly because I was benefiting a "needy" person.

I cringed, thinking how mad that would have made Shirley, who always said she didn't "need nothin' from nobody." As for me, the whole Turn-Off-the-Tube report had turned out to be a big disappointment. I didn't even want to think about it.

The only good thing, now that school was over, was that I'd have a lot more time to go around collecting trash with Shirley Brummage. I still didn't know her very well. I didn't even know where she lived because I usually met her on whichever street she went rummaging through that day of the week. And I *still* didn't know what she was doing with all those coupons I was cutting out and turning over to her.

So far, though, things hadn't been working out as I'd hoped, because my mother had all sorts of other ideas for my summer vacation. She had started doing the "spring" housecleaning that she hadn't had a chance to do when Grandma Florence was with us. And she wanted me to help—straightening up my room, cleaning out drawers and closets, and most of all getting the guest room ready for Daphne, who was coming at the end of next week.

"I have an idea, Pammy. What do you think if I put the portable black-and-white TV from our bedroom into her room? Wouldn't that make her feel nice and welcome? Her own little set to be cozy with?"

"Why should she have her 'own little set'?" I wanted to know. "I don't have my own. I never did."

"Because you don't care that much about TV, Pam. You proved it when you did that experiment for school. And I don't even see you watching the color set in the den much these days."

"That's because you hardly give me a moment to breathe. Do this, do that. And all this fixing up the guest room for Daffy—I mean, Daff-nee. You'd think the queen was coming. You didn't even fuss that much over Grandma Florence."

"That's not true," my mother said. She was sitting at the sewing machine, running up a new dust ruffle for Daphne's bed out of a pretty, flower-printed bedsheet that she'd bought specially. "Anyhow, a guest *should* be treated like royalty. That's what hospitality is all about."

"But she's only a kid. Like me," I complained. "Even if she is eleven and a half. So what if she's coming all the way from California? Is that what makes her so special?"

My mother kept her head bent and concentrated on the gathers she was making in the dust ruffle.

"And what are she and I supposed to *do* all summer?" I nagged on. "Did you ever think of that?"

"We'll think of all sorts of things to do once we find out what she's interested in. It'll be fun showing her around. What would you do if she weren't coming?"

"Plenty," I said, thinking of Shirley and hoping I'd be able to catch her tomorrow in the neighborhood where she usually went collecting on Thursdays.

My mother finished the row of gathers and held it up to admire it. "There!" Then she added absently, "For a start, you can introduce Daphne to your friends and you can take her along with you when you do 'plenty.' "

I pressed my lips together in exasperation. Was my mother getting fuzzy-headed or something? Had she flipped out from the strain of having Grandma Florence around? "*My* friends and Daphne," I reminded her, "are not the same *age*."

"Well," she remarked, "they probably have older sisters and brothers. Something will turn up, I'm sure."

I curled my hands into fists and dug my knuckles into my sides. "I just wish you'd tell me," I said, "the real reason she's coming here for the summer. There's something very sneaky and suspicious about this whole business."

My mother gave me an innocent smile. "I've already told you, Pammy. It's so you'll get the feeling of what it's like to have a sister, someone near your own age to share experiences with, to help you learn to give a little. You can't always be the single shining star. It's not . . . healthy."

"Oh, so that's what you think of me," I said, suddenly feeling close to tears.

She reached out and put her arms around me. "Don't be upset, Pammy. Your father and I really talked this through. We can't give you a sister or brother of your own. And I know you said you didn't want one anyway. But someday you'll go out into the real world and you won't find it so easy to get along with people. They'll think you're too bossy. You won't always get your own way. You'll be put down time after time. You'll have lots of disappointments."

"What do I care?" I shrugged. It had already happened to me at the end of fourth grade. My Turn-Off-the-Tube report was the best, but Ms. Babcock and the kids in the class just wouldn't admit it. I hadn't even told my mother about that disappointment. So what?

I narrowed my eyes. "And is that the only reason Daphne, the queen from California, is coming to spend the summer with us?"

"Ummm hmm," my mother nodded blithely.

"It's still a weird idea," I insisted. "I guess you already realize I'm probably going to hate her."

8 Daphne was supposed to arrive a couple of days after the Fourth of July. My father took the afternoon off and we all drove to the airport.

"Hey," I shouted from the backseat when we were about halfway there, "how will we know her? Does anybody have any idea what she looks like?"

"Calm down, Pammy," my mother replied. "There can't be that many eleven-and-a-half-year-old girls traveling all by themselves. Besides, one of the flight attendants will know all about her and will see that she's delivered to us personally."

Just like a special-delivery package, I thought. *Or* a newborn baby.

I just hoped Daphne wouldn't turn out to be one of those la-di-da types, tall and tanned, with long blond hair, who drooled over boys, treated me like an obnoxious kid sister, and maybe even smoked pot. Had my mother ever thought about *that!*

Or maybe she'd be one of those pale-looking characters who ate only brown rice and vegetables, sat cross-legged and chanted for hours, did yoga exercises, and looked down her nose at people who "killed" for their food.

Daphne was a "surprise," after all. And that could mean anything.

As soon as we got inside the terminal building at the airport, I began spotting all kinds of kids around Daphne's age who could have been her—sixth-graders who really thought they had it made. But of course it was silly of me to be looking at them, because Daphne's plane hadn't even landed yet.

My mother kept dashing around checking up on the arrival gate and my father acted even calmer than usual, which was always a bad sign.

"Why's Mom so nervous?" I asked him, as we followed her scurrying figure to gate 11A after a last-minute change from gate 14B.

My father rested a large, warm hand on the back of my neck. It was hard to tell if it was meant to be a comfort or a warning. "This is a big responsibility for her, Pamela. We expect full cooperation from you. Don't forget to do your part."

I was about to say, "Why? I never asked for her to come here." But at that moment we saw my mother waving frantically to us from a whole bunch of people and calling out, "Sid! Pamela! The plane's just in."

A large metal door swung open into the arrival lounge and passengers began dribbling in, very slowly at first, from the telescoped walkway connecting the plane and the terminal building. The first person off was an old woman in a wheelchair being pushed by another woman, then a red-faced man with a briefcase, a young mother with a baby and a little kid, a stewardess—by herself—followed by more grown-ups, a young bearded man with a guitar. . . .

My mother glanced worriedly at my father. "I thought she'd be one of the first ones off the plane."

"Maybe she missed it," I said hopefully. "Maybe it's the wrong plane. Maybe . . ."

Whole clots of people began getting off now. It was hard to sort them out. My mother was staring intensely into the crowd, and my father was keeping his eye on the doorway. Suddenly there was a tap on my shoulder and I looked up into the eyes of a blankly smiling, sandy-haired stewardess.

"Teitelbaum?"

"That's us," I answered. And my parents both turned around at once.

"Oh. Here she is!" my mother exclaimed.

The stewardess had sort of reached around behind her and produced . . . Daphne.

I blinked. She was a short girl, not a whole lot taller than I was, still with plenty of baby fat on her face and body, and with long, curly dark hair and very pink cheeks. She smiled vaguely like somebody in a dream and I noticed that her eyes were a deep violet with long, thick lashes.

"She was asleep," the stewardess was explaining. "She slept most of the trip, so I was sure she'd be awake for the landing. But when I went back to get her, she was still dozing in her seat, which is why we were so late getting off."

Daphne yawned and stretched and smiled some more.

"Well, anyway, better late than never," the stewardess said perkily as she handed Daphne's small traveling bag to my father.

We all headed for the baggage claim to get Daphne's suitcases. All she and I had been doing so far was looking at each other and smiling, while Daphne continued to yawn a lot. I noticed that she had perfect white teeth and lips that were naturally rosy. She was as pretty as Snow White in a little kid's picture book. But was she ever going to wake up and act alive?

"What are you, real tired or something?" I asked her as we watched the empty baggage carrousel going around and around. She just went on smiling and said, "Ummm."

At last the baggage came off the plane and we

picked up Daphne's. Then we all got into the car and drove home. On the way, Daphne fell asleep again, huddled in her corner of the backseat.

I leaned forward, tapped my mother on the shoulder and whispered to her. She turned and looked at Daphne's gracefully sleeping form. Then she put her finger on her lips and smiled.

I bounced back into my corner and frowned out the window. In one way, I guess I was sort of relieved. But I was also puzzled. I wasn't sure what I'd been expecting Daphne to be like. But one thing I knew for certain. I wasn't expecting the Sleeping Beauty.

"Mom, can I go out and play?"

It was the next afternoon, and Daphne was lying on her little white bed with the pretty dust ruffle, looking like a rumpled life-size doll and watching TV.

"What's Daphne doing?"

"She's watching a soap opera or maybe it's a movie, I'm not sure. She says she's tired and wants to rest."

My mother ran her hand through her hair. "What could be wrong with that child?"

"She has sleeping sickness. She wants to spend the whole summer watching TV and sleeping. What's wrong with that?"

"It's unnatural," my mother said. "Even Grandma Florence didn't sleep that much after she had her operation. All Daphne had was a plane trip. She shouldn't be that knocked out."

"I told you we shouldn't have any more sleep-over company. It's unlucky."

"Oh Pammy, such nonsense. Tell me what you and she talked about when you went out together this morning."

"Nothing. I told you. She won't talk. We walked around the neighborhood. I showed her my school. She said, 'That's nice.' I showed her the park, we went by the tennis courts, the swimming pool. She said, 'That's nice, that's nice.' We met Sharon Marple wheeling her baby brother and sister around. I told Daphne, 'That's a girl in my class who has a lot of little kids in her family.' She said, 'That's nice.' "

"Do you think she's homesick?"

Daphne had talked to her mother in California on the phone last night and gone to sleep right afterward.

"Nah, she probably acts like that at home, too. She's just . . . limp. Maybe if we could put her in the blender and whirl her around a little . . . Listen, I really have to go out and meet a friend of mine. Can I?"

"Yes, Pammy. But be back in an hour. I don't

70

want her 'resting' up there all afternoon. One hour."

Free at last, I raced out to start searching around town for Shirley Brummage.

It wasn't easy. I hadn't seen Shirley for days, and the last time she'd acted kind of standoffish. Did she think I didn't *want* to see her?

After I'd tried a few of the streets where I thought she might be, I went over to the business part of town and asked for her at the antique shop and then at one of the used-furniture stores. "Haven't seen her in a while," the people I asked both told me. "Weather's probably too warm for an old gal like her to be gallivanting around," said the man at the used-furniture store.

Even though it wasn't Wednesday, I thought I'd try the library because it was air-conditioned. But when I asked somebody the time, I found out my hour was already up, so I headed back home.

Daphne was in the kitchen eating a Popsicle from the freezer. My mother gave me a bright look as if to show how proud she was of getting Daphne down from her room.

"Just in time," she said. "I want you and Daphne to go to the store for me." She put a list in front of me. "Get all these items, and also

71

Daphne's going to pick up her favorite breakfast cereal and some other things we don't have that she likes to eat."

I washed up a little and we started out for the supermarket that was closest to home. Daphne was quiet and dreamy as usual.

"So how do you like it here so far?" I asked her.

"Oh, it's okay."

"Is it different from where you live in California?"

"Not much."

"What grade are you going into next?"

"Seventh."

"Do you like school?"

"It's okay."

"Do you still feel tired from the plane trip?"

"Not much."

I was really getting exasperated. Daphne had about three answers, all two words long. She never spoke a whole sentence and she never asked any questions at all.

I decided to try one more new subject before we got to the store.

"Do you watch a whole lot of TV at home, too?"

"Um hmmm."

"Why?"

"I like it."

"I can live without it," I told her. "I didn't turn on the tube once in three whole weeks. We were having this experiment at school. . . ." And I told her about the Turn-Off-the-Tube project, not mentioning my report or how it had come in second best, because I was still angry at Ms. Babcock over that.

Daphne listened and at first I thought she was going to say, "That's nice."

Instead, she actually began to talk in sentences. "Oh, I love TV," she said. "It's better than the real world. It's even better than the dreams you dream when you're asleep. Because in TV you can *pick* your dreams—I mean, your programs. And if you want a scary one that day, you can have it. But if you don't, you can have something real soothing or romantic. Or funny. Or whatever."

It was my turn to say, "Hmmm." After thinking a while, I said, "Is that why you always either sleep or watch TV? Because you don't like to be in the real world?"

"Um hmmm," Daphne said dreamily. "Because the real world, you know"—she mulled around for the right word—"it stinks."

9 The first thing I saw when we got inside the supermarket was a little beat-up kid's wagon. It was parked right next to the manager's office.

I forgot all about Daphne and went straight over there. I planted my arms on the countertop beside the office and hoisted myself up to look deeper inside the glassed cubicle, which was just to the right. Sure enough, there at his desk was the store manager and with him was Shirley Brummage. She was wearing dark glasses that I'd never seen on her before—she usually just squinted a lot—and she had on a saggy-looking dress with a belt made out of fuzzy rope and her usual sneakers.

I could hear the manager talking through the open doorway. "Shirley," he was saying in a patient voice, "I can't use all of these. Lots of them are for products I don't carry. And some of them I've got too many of already. For example, how much of this brand of frozen pizza do you think I sell in a half a year?"

Just then the telephone rang and the store manager picked it up.

74

"Psst," I called softly.

Shirley looked up in alarm. She bounded over to the high counter from which I was still dangling. "Not now, Pieface, not now," she whispered. "I got business here. Can't ya see?"

"Yeah, okay," I said. "I'll stick around, though. Don't go away without me."

I got down and turned to find Daphne standing there with an empty shopping cart she had just corralled.

"Who was *that?*" she asked, making a face.

Good. At last Daphne had asked a question. Her first one.

"She's a friend of mine," I said coolly as we set off down the aisle where the dry cereals were.

"Isn't she a little old for you?" Another question. Great.

"I don't pick my friends by age," I told her. "Listen, I can't let her leave without talking to her about something. You take the grocery list. I might have to scoot off at any moment."

I kept looking behind me, not wanting to go too deep into the store. Finally I left Daphne with the shopping cart and went back to the manager's office. I boosted myself up onto the counter again to peek into the room.

This time I saw the store manager scoop up a whole bunch of grocery coupons from his desk and toss them into a drawer. Then he opened a little metal box and began counting out money to Shirley.

Shirley got up from her chair and reached for the money. She undid a safety pin, tucked the bills into one of the pockets of her dress, and then fastened the top of the pocket to the dress with the safety pin. "See ya again," she said brightly.

The manager had gotten up from his desk and was following Shirley out of the office, one hand resting on her shoulder.

"Yeah, okay. But listen, honey, don't overload me. Try to get yourself a few other stores. You've got to spread this stuff around, you know. It's understandable that folks in certain neighborhoods would go in more for cashing in discount coupons. But not all at one store, see?"

Shirley nodded. "Sure. Gotcha."

At that moment she spotted me, standing a little distance from the manager's office. Her eyes shot off a few yellow sparks and she bared her teeth as if she were getting ready to snarl.

I backed away and waited until she'd taken her wagon and walked off toward the fruit and vegetable department. The manager had disappeared in the direction of the meat department.

In the fruit department, Shirley began picking through some squashed tomatoes that were sitting on a special table where there were old and damaged vegetables for sale. I figured it was safe to talk to her now.

"Wow," I said, "I've been looking for you all over. Did you know that?"

She looked at me suspiciously. "You been followin' me around, huh?"

"No," I said. "I just found you here by accident. Honest. Say, are you mad at me or something?"

She squeezed a tomato and some juice and seeds spurted out of it. "Too soft," she remarked, putting it back. "No, I ain't mad at you. Just don't like people checkin' up on me, that's all. What I do with those coupons is my business. Told you that a long time ago."

"I wasn't checking up, though," I protested. "And I didn't understand all that stuff about the coupons anyway."

"Good," she said. "Glad to hear it."

Just then along came Daphne pushing the shopping cart with quite a lot of groceries in it. "Oh, there you are," she said, looking faintly annoyed. "I thought you got lost or something."

Shirley glanced up sharply. "And who's this one?"

I explained about Daphne and introduced

her to Shirley. Shirley grunted and Daphne smiled and yawned. Maybe she always did that when she met somebody new.

It turned out Daphne had picked up most of the groceries we needed and Shirley only had to buy a few things—some half-price vegetables, some soup bones with meat on them that she said the butcher always saved for her, a big box of oatmeal, and a big box of dried milk powder. We checked out and put all the packages in Shirley's wagon and started walking home, because Shirley said she was going in the same direction we were. I was pulling the wagon because I was the shortest one of the three of us.

"Whoa," Shirley called out from behind as we came to a small, broken-down apartment house not far from the supermarket. "Here's where you kids get off."

I looked at the dirty brick building with street-level windows that had heavy iron gates on them. Just ahead of us was a sloping walk of cracked cement that turned off and seemed to go down under the apartment house. It was probably where they stored the garbage cans.

"Are you going down there to hunt for trash?" I asked Shirley. She and I had never visited this place before.

"Naw," she said indignantly. "I live here."

"What? Down *there*?" I was sorry right away that I'd said it in that tone.

"Yup. Got the old coal stoker's rooms. Not bad. And cheap. *Dirt* cheap. Ha ha. That's supposed to be a joke. Get it?"

"Could we . . . could we come down and see it?" I asked timidly as long as Shirley seemed to be in such a good mood.

"Suit yerselves," she said, taking the handle of the wagon from me and starting down the walkway.

I glanced at Daphne and she shrugged. Our groceries were still in the wagon anyway, so we just followed Shirley down to the bottom. The walkway turned to the right and there was a dark alcove with a door in it that Shirley opened with two different keys.

We followed her into a dim but very cool room, a sort of kitchen with an easy chair and a TV in it. That room opened into another much larger room that faced onto the street. It had a brass four-poster bed in it and a lot of other big, old pieces of furniture. It was only a little brighter in there because that was the room with the barred windows that looked out onto the sidewalk.

Shirley pulled a chain, and a bright fluorescent ceiling lamp came on in the kitchen. We all blinked.

"It's only dark in the daytime, m'dears," Shirley said jovially. "At night, it's just like anyplace else."

Shirley lifted her bag of groceries out of the wagon.

"It's really kind of nice," I said, peering into the bedroom again.

"No, it ain't," Shirley said. "It's just sort of okay. For me, that is."

To my surprise Daphne asked, "Do you live here all by yourself?"

"You bet," Shirley said gruffly. "I had a family once. But my old man died and my kids all walked out on me. Don't never see 'em nor hear from 'em. Don't never expect I will, neither."

I was surprised. In all the time I'd known Shirley Brummage, she'd never told me anything about herself. Even now, she seemed to be talking only to Daphne.

"That's funny," Daphne said. "My parents walked out on *me* when I was a baby. I never saw them or heard from them in my entire life. And I don't suppose I ever will, either."

I frowned at Daphne. "What are you talking about, anyway? Your parents are in Calif . . ."

Daphne was shaking her head. "Uh-uh. Didn't you know? I'm adopted."

"Of course I didn't know," I answered, getting annoyed and embarrassed. "Nobody told me. What am I supposed to be, a mind reader or something?"

"I'd a known in a minute," said Shirley. "We folks c'n always spot one another."

"Oh," I said, beginning to feel hurt now. "What are you, some kind of a private club or something?"

"Yeah," Shirley agreed. "Yeah, you could put it that way, Pieface."

"Let's go," I told Daphne. "It's getting late."

Daphne looked at our grocery packages still sitting in the wagon. "We have a lot to carry," she sighed. "We should have brought a wagon of our own."

"Aw, take that one, Daphne," Shirley said nicely. "You can return it to me tomorrow mornin'. I won't be needin' it before then."

I couldn't get over how pleasantly Shirley was behaving to Daphne. Shirley was supposed to be *my* friend. I was beginning to feel left out.

On the way home, as we were taking turns pulling the wagon, Daphne turned to me and actually asked me another question.

"How come she calls you Pieface and she calls me Daphne?"

I had been thinking about that, too.

"I don't know," I answered grumpily after a while. "But I have an idea it's because she likes you *better* than me."

81

10 My mother decided that Daphne should meet the rest of our family.

"A very good way to do it," she said, "would be for us to give a bridal shower for Lainie."

My mother and I were in the kitchen, where I was helping fix a picnic lunch for Daphne and me to take to the park. Daphne was upstairs in her room watching TV.

"That way," my mother went on, half thinking out loud, "we could get most of the relatives from *that* side of the family together."

"Including Grandma Florence," I reminded her.

"Including Grandma Florence, of course," she said, as naturally as if nothing at all had happened at the end of Grandma Florence's last visit.

Actually, I didn't care one way or the other whether Daphne met the rest of the family. But I did love the idea of the party. I hadn't seen my cousin Lainie since she had rearranged the wedding ceremony so that I could be a flower girl, and I was starting to count the days until I'd be walking down the aisle in front of her while everybody looked on breathlessly.

"It will be a lot of work," my mother said thoughtfully. "Maybe thirty or forty people." My mother's family was small and scattered, but my father's was really big. "But I think it might help Daphne to feel more . . . part of things. It would give her a sense of . . . family."

"Oh," I said, slightly annoyed. "You're doing it for her, then? Why? Just because she's adopted?"

My mother looked up from wrapping a sandwich. There was a stunned expression on her face. "How did you find out?"

"Daphne told me."

I couldn't explain that I'd found out right in front of Shirley Brummage, or how embarrassed I'd been. Because I still hadn't gotten around to telling my mother anything *about* Shirley Brummage.

My mother frowned. "The poor child. How did she say it? Was she upset?"

"No. *I* was. You know I hate secrets and being the last person to find out about something. You should have let me know."

"Yes," my mother agreed slowly. "I suppose I should have. I didn't want to color your feelings, though. And I didn't know if Daphne would want to talk about it. I'm glad she wasn't upset. I'm glad she accepts it so naturally."

"I don't know if she does, though," I said. "She told me that she hates the 'real world.' She says it . . . 'stinks.'"

My mother winced.

"She says that's why she watches so much TV. And I also happen to think that's why she sleeps so much."

My mother sighed deeply and shook her head. "Oh, Pammy, the awful things that parents can do to children."

I was puzzled. "It happened a long time ago, though. Personally, I think she's one of those kids who's hooked for life on TV. And she's probably using all this adoption business as an excuse."

My mother was standing at the sink now with her back to me. "Don't be too sure," she said. "There might be complications."

"Like what?" I wanted to know.

"O-h-h," she said mysteriously, "just . . . complications."

"This whole thing is getting to sound like a soap opera," I remarked. "Maybe *you're* watching too much TV, too."

After I got the lunch all packed up, I had to wait for Daphne's program to end. She always had to see the last little bit of every commercial. Then she'd finally sit up straight, rub her eyes, smile, and yawn. It was as though she was slowly coming out of a dream.

At last, I got her to get her swimming things together for the park pool, and I dragged her out of the house.

"It isn't fair, you know," I said, as Daphne and I started walking, "that I have to do everything. Plan what we should do for the day, make the lunch. The other morning, *I* had to take the wagon back to Shirley Brummage. She wasn't even glad to see me. 'Where's Daphne?' she asked me. So I told her the truth. 'Daphne's watching TV. She can't miss her favorite program.' Only *every* program's your favorite program," I added sarcastically. "I honestly don't see why I bother to try to see you're entertained."

"Well, don't then," she said calmly. "I told you I'd be perfectly happy up in my room."

"My mother cares," I continued irritably. "I don't. I would just let you stay there all summer. I have plenty of friends I could be having fun with."

"Like that Shirley what's-her-name?"

"Plenty," I repeated.

We got to the pool. It was a hot day, and the pool was crowded. I was so annoyed with Daphne by then that I decided I wasn't going to wait around for her to get ready. She was poky about everything. So, as soon as I was in my bathing suit, I left her in the girls' changing room and went out to the pool and jumped right in.

The water felt great, and I must have splashed around for about ten minutes. It was almost impossible to swim because the pool was practically wall-to-wall people. After a while, I decided I'd better find Daphne, so I began paddling around looking for her. I thought I'd seen her pack a red-and-blue bathing suit and a white bathing cap. A couple of kids in white bathing caps got real mad when I came up behind them, grabbed their shoulders, and twisted their heads around to see if they were Daphne. None of them were, though.

I decided to get out of the pool so I could have a better view of what was going on down there in the water. It was a mess, really. Screaming, splashing, squirming, jumping, and leaping bodies. I didn't even know what Daphne looked like in a bathing suit. Maybe she hadn't even gone into the water yet. Knowing how she always took her time, that was very possible.

I started walking all around the pool to see if she was sitting or standing along the edge. I went all the way to the very deep end where the lifeguard sat. No Daphne anywhere. So I went back to the other end, stepped up close to the rim of the pool, cupped my hands around my mouth, and bawled out as loud as I could, "DAFF-NEE!"

After I'd done that about five or six times, hoping she'd be able to hear me over all the noise, a skinny kid with his hair plastered down over his eyes climbed out of the pool and came toward me.

"I might have known," he said, pushing his hair away and rubbing the water out of his eyes. "The great Pamela Teitelbaum, yelling her head off as usual."

"Oh," I said, in a flat voice. "It's you."

"Who'd you expect?" Phil Barber asked. "A mermaid?"

I stepped away from him, deciding I'd go over to another part of the pool and yell some more.

"Who is this 'Daff-nee,' anyway?" Phil asked, following me and flicking droplets of water at my back.

I ignored him and went through the same routine as before. A couple of kids in the pool had started to mimic me and some others had begun to shout, "Aw, cut it out."

"What's so important?" Phil wanted to know. "Did your cat drown or are you just trying to get attention, like always?"

"Very funny," I snapped. "Daphne's not a cat."

I started for the changing room. Daphne was probably still in there. Maybe she'd found a TV set. I'd just remembered that the matron had one in a little room off to the side. She watched in there on slow days.

When I came out, Phil was still standing where I'd left him.

"She's not in there, either." I was beginning to get kind of worried.

"Who? Who? Who?" Phil asked, shaking his hands so they looked like flopping white fish.

"Daphne," I began. "My . . . cousin. From California." I didn't think of her as my "cousin," but it didn't feel right saying "my friend," either. Daphne and I weren't friends. We were just sort of putting up with one another.

Phil actually listened with a serious expression while I explained about how she and I had come to the park together with a picnic lunch and our swimming things.

He poked a finger in his ear to release some water. "I think you should go tell the lifeguard, Pamela. Maybe they could have the pool dragged."

"No," I said emphatically. I could just see them ordering everybody out of the pool. If

Daphne didn't turn up, I'd feel silly. If, on the other hand . . . If she was lying there at the bottom, drowned . . .

"You've got to," Phil insisted. "If you don't tell him, I will. You could be held responsible. You should have kept your eye on the kid."

"She's not a . . . a kid. She's two years older than I am," I informed him. "And she said she knew how to swim."

"She could have gotten a cramp," Phil said. "Or maybe some other kid knocked her on the head by accident and she went down. The pool's so crowded today, anything could happen."

"Oh, all right," I agreed reluctantly.

We marched over toward the lifeguard's station. The stocky, golden-skinned lifeguard was standing at the base of his tall perch and chatting with one of the uniformed town policemen who was always on duty in the park. They stopped talking and stared at us.

"Ye-e-s," said the cop. "You kids got a problem?"

I flashed a resentful look at Phil. Because of him I now had to explain the whole thing to the police.

"We think my . . . uh, cousin might be in the pool," I reported quickly.

The cop glanced down the whole length of

the jam-packed swimming pool and I thought I saw him smile.

"Not on the top where you can see her," I added. "On the bottom. Maybe."

"Oh-oh. Job for you, Josh," the cop said, turning to the lifeguard.

The lifeguard tore off his sunglasses. "What part of the pool did you see her in last?" he inquired.

I looked at Phil again. How could I say, "I didn't see her in the pool at all—the last time I saw her was in the girls' changing room"? It was all Phil's fault. I began to stammer, "Well, uh, she . . ."

"Never mind," Josh said quickly. "Let's check it out. Time's awastin'."

Without another word, he dived in off the deep end and vanished beneath the surface of the water.

11 I stood in the hot sunshine at the edge of the pool and started shivering. All the thoughts Phil Barber had put into my mind about how Daphne could have sunk to the bottom and not come up began to dance around like devils. It really would be my fault if something happened to her. I'd been picking on her awfully, I supposed. But, honestly, I'd been getting so fed up with that "sad princess" act of hers.

Of course, I couldn't be sure it was an act. She didn't actually mope or complain. She just looked pretty and acted quiet. And somehow people got to thinking that she was so sweet and so unhappy, and started worrying about cheering her up and making her feel at home. Even Shirley Brummage, who was so tough and could be so mean-sounding, softened up when it came to Daphne. Why? Why didn't anybody ever act that way toward me?

The park policeman clapped a heavy hand on my shoulder, and I jumped.

"Take it easy now, sis. We don't get more than one drowning every five or six years here.

Chances are your cousin's splashing around down at the other end with the rest of them."

I looked up at him. He had a deeply lined face and a thin mouth that looked like a lopsided slash mark across his face. But his voice was soft, almost gentle.

"Thing is," he went on, "if Josh doesn't come up with anything in the pool area, we ought to find out where she did go. How old is she? About your age?"

I told him how old Daphne was and explained how she was visiting us from California, never taking my eyes off the water once. Josh had already surfaced a couple of times and gone right down again.

At last he came up waving and grinning.

"Not a trace," he said. "Here's all I found." He held out a clenched fist to me. "Wouldn't be hers, I don't suppose."

I stared at the fist as it opened to reveal a single gold hoop earring.

I shook my head. "Daphne didn't wear earrings." There was a catch in my throat.

"Okay," Josh said cheerfully. "Don't give up. We'll check some more. Now, what's her full name?"

About ten minutes later, after Josh had blown his whistle and gotten the attention of every kid in the pool, and after the matron had done a thorough search of the girls' changing room *and* the bathroom *and* the first-aid hut, the policeman and I set off into the park itself.

Phil Barber, who had been hanging around the whole time, said, "Phew, I hope you find her. It sure doesn't look good. Listen, phone me later, Pamela, and let me know what happens."

"Oh, sure," I said sourly, as I watched him jump back into the pool with a terrific splash.

"Now, think hard," the cop was saying. "Is there some chance she could have taken off for home, gone off in a huff? Did you kids have a fight or anything?"

"Uh-uh," I assured him. "No fight. And it's about eight blocks from here to our house. I'm not even sure she'd know the way. Besides, my mother said she was going out shopping. So Daphne couldn't even get in."

We were walking across a sloping grassy part of the park that was beginning to turn yellowish brown because there hadn't been much rain lately. A path ran through this part, but the benches alongside it were all empty because of the hot sunshine.

"Quiet over here," the cop commented. "A little too quiet. See those trees over past the benches? Now, that's a little dangerous when there's no one around. Like today. Or, say, late at night. Now and then we get a little incident

93

in there. Don't want to scare you, but you kids should learn to operate by the buddy system. Keep in twos at least. Not saying it's a sure way, but it's a lot safer than any kid going off on her own."

I nodded. It seemed a dumb place for anyone to go. The picnic grove was over on the other side of the pool. It had trees and tables and even a few grills for cookouts.

"Let's take a look in that thick clump of trees," the cop suggested. "Keep my conscience clear."

"I think . . ." I said slowly, "that where she'd go would be anywhere there was a television set. See, she's hooked on TV, sort of like a dope . . ."

"Addict?"

"Yup. That's it. And she can't stay away from the tube too long. She starts to go . . ."

"Bonkers."

"Yup. Like that. So, maybe . . ."

We had crossed over now to the grove of trees. The ground in between the thick trunks was soft and spongy, covered with thin grass or moss, and it was cool and dim in there, with only little dapples and streaks of sunlight.

We began circling the trees. The cop would loop around one way and I'd loop around another. Then we'd crisscross each other and go off in opposite directions again. This was like some silly game. What was he expecting to find in here—the big, bad wolf; Little Red Riding Hood? I kept thinking it would make a lot more sense to sniff out the nearest television set. And there, glued to the tube, just about for certain, would be . . .

"Daphne!"

I gasped her name in a shocked, raspy whisper. She was lying on the ground at the foot of a huge tree. Her beach bag with her bathing suit and towel in it was propped up under her head. Her eyes were shut. Almost.

I crept closer and, from underneath her long lashes, I could just see the tiniest bit of white of eye glimmering. What did the policeman mean that it was "dangerous" in here, that every now and then they had a "little incident"? Was Daphne asleep? Had she fainted? Or was she . . .?

"DAFF-NEE!" I shouted. "Wake up this minute."

The cop came running. "You found her. *Don't* touch her." He quickly knelt down beside her stretched-out figure.

Daphne began to open her eyes slowly. She saw me and she smiled. Then, of course, she yawned.

"You all right, sis? What happened to you?

Can you talk?" the policeman asked.

"Sure she can talk," I told him, feeling myself stiffen with anger. "As soon as she stops yawning."

The cop looked up at me in disbelief. "You mean to tell me she wandered off here all by herself and *fell asleep?*"

"Sure," I said. "Just like Sleeping Beauty. I should have told you. That's the other thing she's hooked on. If she can't watch television, she goes to sleep."

Daphne was sitting up now and brushing herself off. "Gosh, I'm hungry, Pamela. Have you got the lunch with you? What time is it?"

The cop pushed his cap back and scratched his forehead. "Well, I never." He grabbed Daphne by her shoulders and pulled her to her feet. "You on any kind of stuff, kid? Better tell me. I can find out in a jiffy."

Daphne shook her head. Her cheeks and lips were rosy with sleep, her eyes were drowsy and innocent.

"I'm fine, really," she said. "It was just so awfully crowded at the pool and it was so hot in the sun. So I thought I'd come over here and lie down and rest until lunchtime."

I stood there with my arms folded across my chest, trying not to scream.

"So why didn't you tell me that's what you

were going to do? Do you know they were looking for you all over the pool, even at the bottom? And then they tried the locker room and the bathroom and the first-aid station. And I was really worried about you."

"I *couldn't* tell you," Daphne said calmly, "because I couldn't find you. You disappeared on me."

"Oh," I challenged. "So then *you* decided to disappear, too. All the way over here. Where hardly anybody would ever *think* of looking for you."

Daphne shrugged one shoulder. "Well, I just thought as long as you disappeared . . ."

"Baloney!" I burst out. "You *knew* I was in the pool. You did it for spite! You always act so innocent." I made a mocking face. "Always so sweet and helpless and innocent. Just to make me look like the bad one all the time. But I know you. You're nothing but a . . . a phony." I shot a fist out at Daphne. "I ought to punch you right in the—"

Daphne shrieked softly and ran behind a tree. The cop caught both my arms and pinned them to my body.

"Now see here, kids. No fighting. . . ."

He looked down at me grimly. "I asked you before if you two kids had had a fight. You told me no. I been in this business awhile, so why'd you try to fool me? What'd you tell me no for?"

"Because we didn't. Then. That's the truth. You can even ask *her*," I said exasperatedly, trying to keep my lower lip from trembling and pointing to Daphne, who was peeking out from behind the tree.

"Okay, okay," the cop said in a calmer voice. "I got two daughters of my own at home. Well, they're grown up now. But I can remember how it used to be."

"We aren't sisters," I said sharply. "We aren't even cousins, in fact."

"Oh no?" he said with some interest. "I thought you told me you were."

Daphne was approaching timidly. "Our . . . mothers are. Cousins."

The cop nodded. "Same thing. Almost." He smiled really fondly at Daphne. "You seem like a nice enough kid. But since you two aren't getting along too well, tell you what we're gonna do." He turned to me with a hard look. "You're going back to the pool and get changed, get all your stuff out of the locker, and I'll call a patrol car to drive you both home. *After* I phone and make sure there's somebody at home to referee you two."

Half an hour later, Daphne and I were being driven to our house in a police car, with our uneaten lunch sitting on the seat between us.

I'd decided I wasn't talking to Daphne. Ever again. But I didn't know if she knew it yet. She was gazing out the window dreamily. And, I swear, she was smiling.

12 I found Shirley Brummage at a one-day flea market that was being held in the back parking lot of the shopping center. I figured that was where she'd be because she told me she always went to flea markets to unload the odds and ends she couldn't sell to dealers or couldn't get a good enough price for.

It was about ten o'clock in the morning and already very hot and sunny. Shirley was sitting on a little wooden folding stool with a big black umbrella propped up over her head. Her wagon, with the things she wanted to sell, was parked at her feet.

"Hi," I said eagerly. "Say, I'm really glad to see you."

It would be a break for me to be able to spend an entire day away from Daphne *and* from my mother's angry looks about the way I'd been acting.

Since the police car had brought Daphne and me home from the park a week ago, I was just sort of grunting instead of talking to anyone, and slinking out whenever I could. One afternoon, my mother had taken Daphne out to lunch and clothes shopping with her. But most of the time, Daphne was back to watching TV up in her room. I didn't care. I was glad the mess-up in the park had happened. Because now I was really finished with having anything to do with Daphne.

"You all by yerself?" Shirley squinted from under the umbrella. She wasn't wearing the dark sunglasses I'd seen on her in the supermarket. Probably she'd found them somewhere and maybe she'd already sold them that morning at the flea market. Also, the folding stool and the umbrella were most likely somebody's throw-outs that she'd found in the trash.

"Yup," I said, trying to sound cheerful. "Who'd you expect?"

"Where's Daphne?"

"I knew it. I knew you'd ask me about her first thing. She's home watching TV. I already told you she'd rather do that than anything else."

"Kid oughtta get out more," Shirley commented.

I stuck my hands on my hips. "I'm through with trying to take her places. Why is everybody so worried about Daphne? I'm just sick of hearing about her and her so-called troubles. Why doesn't somebody ever worry about me?"

"You, Pieface!" Shirley spluttered with laughter. "You're tough as nails. You're all spit 'n' vinegar."

"I'm wh-a-a-t?" I'd never heard that expression before.

"Back off there, now," Shirley hissed, as some customers came dawdling along and poked into Shirley's wagon. She sold them a kid's jump rope and a Japanese flower vase.

"You two kids had a fight, huh?" Shirley said, as she pocketed the money.

"Sort of. Only she won't really come out and fight. She's so sneaky. She gets me all steamed up and makes me say all the bad things. Then I get blamed. And she just smiles. O-o-oh . . ." I was still thinking of the way Daphne had sat in the patrol car. "I could just haul off and sock her one right in the jaw!"

Shirley cackled. "Yeah. You're two-fisted all right. But let me tell ya, one of these days you're gonna look around you and you ain't gonna have no friends, no family, no nobody. Now, I ain't sayin' that's all bad. I'm a loner myself. But you just gotta be prepared for it. Know what you're doin' and don't expect no favors from strangers. See."

I had sat down cross-legged on the ground in the shade of Shirley's umbrella. "Why did your kids run out on you? I never even knew you had any kids till you told Daphne you did. How many? Were they boys or girls?"

Shirley's mouth had clamped shut. And it looked like it was going to stay that way.

"I'll bet you'd talk if Daphne was here. Just answer me that, huh? You would, wouldn't you? It's because you like her better than me, isn't it?"

Shirley shook her head. "Feel sorry for her. She's all huddled up inside herself. Comes from gittin' hurt and scared. I know the feelin'."

"You?" I said. "You're nothing like Daphne. Did your parents run out on you, too? Your parents *and* your kids. Both?"

"My business," Shirley said stubbornly. "I told you that first time I met you, Pieface. I got my business. You got yours. Mind it."

"And that's another thing," I said heatedly. "Why do you always call me Pieface when you know my name is Pamela? You always call Daphne Daphne. You never call *her* some dumb name. And I could think of plenty."

"I call her Daphne 'cause it's right for her. Call you Pieface 'cause you got a round face like a pie. Suits ya. With them little dark slits cut in the dough for the steam to come out, just where yer mouth and nose and eyes is."

"Oh yeah? What kind of a pie?"

"Blackberry, I'd say. Tart 'n' spurty. Kind that

gits sticky fruit goo all over the bottom of the oven. Yeah, I used to bake a good pie in my day. That's what Ralph always used to say."

Was Ralph Shirley's husband or her son? It was no use asking her. I knew she wouldn't tell me. I didn't know whether I ought to be sore at Shirley or not. In some ways she and I were a lot alike. So why did she seem to like Daphne so much better than me?

The flea market began to get crowded. More and more people were stopping to pick over the things in Shirley's wagon. She sold a couple of brass lamp chains, an inflatable rubber duck that needed a patch, a curlicued picture frame with a cracked glass in it, and a carving of an elephant with one tusk missing. It was strange the things that some people threw out and that other people bought. I helped Shirley to rearrange the things in her wagon and also to put out some new stuff that she had brought along in a burlap bag that was stowed away behind her.

By now it was getting to be noontime, and Shirley, it turned out, had brought her lunch with her in a paper bag.

"It's sure hot today," she said, starting to gnaw on a strange-looking bone that had some meat hanging off it, and sucking on a squashy tomato.

I knew I was supposed to show up at home for lunch, but I was planning on coming right back to the flea market afterward. I jingled some money I had in my pocket.

"Hey, how about my going over into the shopping center and bringing you back something real cold to drink with your lunch? It'd only take a minute. Then I've got to leave for a while."

Shirley shook her head. "Nah. Tell ya what. I'll go over myself. If you could just stay here and mind the store a few minutes."

"Sure. Why not?"

Shirley put the rest of her lunch back in the paper bag and rolled the top down tightly. Then she leaned one hand on the wagon and started to get up.

"There goes that dang leg again," she mumbled. "Been settin' on this low thing too long." She staggered around a little bit and seemed to reach out for something to steady herself on.

The next instant she bounced down hard onto the stool.

"What's the matter? Want me to help?" I remembered standing next to Grandma Florence's bed in the den and holding out my hands to her so she could grab onto my wrists and ease herself up into a sitting position.

Shirley clutched at my wrists and got to her

feet. Even so, she teetered back and forth. Then she took a wobbly step forward and stopped. She stood still and rocked around like somebody trying to balance herself on a high wire. "Dang, dang, dang!" she muttered through tightly clenched teeth.

Shirley's face had gone almost as gray-white as her hair.

"What is it? Does your leg hurt something awful?"

She glanced down at it furiously. "It don't hurt at all. It's just numb. Numb and a little bit tingly. Can't git the dang thing to move."

"Maybe . . . maybe if you had something to lean on." I looked around quickly. "What about this?" I folded up the big umbrella and gave it to Shirley. She grasped the thick, curved handle and took a few steps, her left leg dragging each time to keep up with her right one.

"Is it better, huh?"

"Yeah, yeah. It's fine, Pieface. Listen, fold up that there stool and pile it in the wagon with the rest of the stuff. Okay?"

"You're leaving?"

"Yeah. Why not. Had a pretty good morning. No use settin' out here in the hot sun all day. Think you can pull that wagon?"

"Sure," I said in a hoarse voice. I picked up the wrinkled paper bag with the rest of Shirley's lunch in it. "What do you think I am? A sissy or something?"

It was nearly past lunchtime when I left Shirley in her apartment. I had helped her into the big brass bed and put the umbrella and an old wooden cane beside it, so she'd have two things to lean on when she got out, in case her leg still wasn't any better.

I'd told her I'd come back after lunch to see how she was, but she'd said, "Nope! Don'tcha dare. The door'll be locked and I'll be sleepin'. Won't be openin' up for nobody. Got that, Pieface? Nobody."

I guess Shirley knew what she was talking about. She said the thing with her leg had happened before. The way she described it, it sounded to me like it had just fallen asleep. I'd had that happen plenty of times—pins and needles, and you had to stamp around a little before your leg woke up. Maybe when it happened to people as old as Shirley, their legs just took a little longer to wake up.

So I hurried home, trying to decide how I'd spend the rest of the afternoon. The park pool, I figured. And this time I wouldn't be taking Daphne with me.

13 The moment I got near the back entrance of our house, I heard a familiar voice. I peeked through the screen door into the kitchen, and sure enough, there was Grandma Florence talking to my mother. She was so sharp-eyed she saw me the instant I saw her.

"Aha! There she is at last. Come give Grandma a kiss."

As usual she grabbed me by the waist, pulling me to her so that I lost my balance. She had certainly gotten her strength back fast since the operation. She looked good, too, with lipstick on and her dark, graying hair freshly set. I think she was even wearing eyebrow pencil and a tiny bit of mascara.

"You look all better," I said.

"I am," she said vigorously. "I've got a whole new lease on life. And look what I brought you, darling."

Sure enough, there was a large flat white box with a ruffly bow lying on the kitchen table. I could already imagine the crinkly tissue paper and all the ruffles nestling inside.

My mother was leaning against the sink with her arms folded. "Where've you been, Pammy? We're waiting lunch for you. Daphne's upstairs getting washed. You'd better get cleaned up, too. Before you even open that package."

My heart sank. That meant we'd all be sitting down to eat together. The table was even set in the dining room.

Upstairs, I met Daphne just coming out of the bathroom. She was wearing a frilly pinafore-style sundress that I hadn't seen on her before. It suited her perfectly.

"That new?" I asked.

"Yes." She smiled. "Your Grandma brought it for me. Wasn't that nice of her? I think you got one, too."

"I'm sure I did," I said, as I closed the bathroom door. It was probably exactly the same dress one size smaller. And it would look terrible on me. Just as terrible as it looked wonderful on Daphne.

"So where were you floating around all morning, sweetie pie?" Grandma Florence wanted to know as soon as we were all seated at the table.

"Oh, I was . . . with a friend," I said, without looking up from my plate.

"You couldn't take Daphne along? What do you think of her? Isn't she some beauty? Such a

109

lovely house guest." Grandma Florence had met Daphne for the first time that morning.

I glanced up at Daphne. She was blushing. Her cheeks were a hot pink, her eyes were cast down, and she had an embarrassed smile on her lips.

"Ma," my mother said playfully to Grandma Florence, "you're making the child self-conscious. Can't you see?"

"Why? Why should she be? Beautiful is beautiful. She'll have plenty of compliments in her life. She might as well get used to it."

Daphne's cheeks flamed even more brightly. I barely suppressed a giggle. My mother cleared her throat and tried to change the subject.

"Grandma and I have been talking about the bridal shower for Lainie. We've set the date, and I'm drafting Pamela and Daphne to work on the invitations and the decorations. We're going to have party tables in the garden and crepe-paper streamers, and the colors will be yellow and white. What do you think?"

I could see my mother was trying hard to get Daphne interested in something besides television, and to get me to become more friendly with Daphne again.

"I can't do it all alone, you know," she went

110

on. "It's going to be a really big party. So do I have a pledge of cooperation from you two?" My mother looked from me to Daphne and back again. Her glance rested sharply, meaningfully, on me.

This was real blackmail, with Grandma Florence looking on and beaming at all of us.

I dipped my head in a nod and grunted, "Okay." I'd get my mother later for this. I loved her, but she was pushing me harder and harder lately. Wasn't she ever going to stop?

Daphne whispered, "Yes," without lifting her lashes.

Grandma Florence's eyes came to rest fondly on Daphne. "I can't get over what a treasure this child is. You know, Evelyn, I would take her to live with me myself. I mean it. Honest."

Daphne raised her eyes for an instant, and I saw a trace of panic in them.

"What are you talking about?" I wanted to know.

I certainly wouldn't have minded if Daphne went to live with Grandma Florence for the rest of the summer. But it did seem kind of an odd thing to happen. Had my mother been telling Grandma Florence how badly I was getting along with Daphne? Was there really a chance?

My mother jumped up quickly from the table.

"Daphne, come and help me with the dessert."

Daphne rose obediently and followed my mother into the kitchen.

I leaned over and clutched Grandma Florence's wrist. "Psst! What do you mean 'take her to live' with you? Would you really? Do you mean right now? How come?" It seemed too good to be true.

Grandma Florence made some little clicking noises with her tongue. "You don't know about the trouble that child is having? Well, you're a little young for such a story, Pamela darling. It's such an upsetting background."

"What is? You mean about her being adopted? I know about that." I didn't see the sense of whispering. "Daphne told me herself."

"Sssh!" Grandma Florence warned, placing a finger on her lips. "That was only the start of it. Now—*eleven* years later—the *adopted* parents are splitting up. Don't tell your mama I told you. She likes everything to be a secret."

I squeezed harder on Grandma Florence's wrist. "What do you mean 'adopted' parents? Which ones are they?"

Grandma Florence waved her head impatiently. "Maybe that's not the right word. I mean the people who adopted her. Your mother's cousin Sandra and her husband. Sandra's a crazy lady, believe me. She was always an extremist." Grandma Florence's voice was rising excitedly. "Now the two of them decide they don't want the marriage anymore; *he* doesn't want the child, *she* doesn't want the child—"

There was a loud crash from the kitchen, like the sound of a whole drawer of silverware falling on the floor. Grandma Florence jumped and pressed her finger to her lips again.

"Sssh. Don't let on I said anything."

My mother and Daphne came into the room carrying plates of ice cream and a tray of cookies. My mother was smiling through tightly clenched teeth, and Daphne never looked up from the cookie tray she was holding. The moment she put it down on the table, she asked if she could be excused because there was a special program she wanted to watch up in her room.

"Of course, dear," my mother said kindly. "Why don't you take your ice cream upstairs with you and eat it while you watch?"

I looked up in shock. My mother had a strict rule about "no eating in the bedrooms." But I knew better than to say anything just then.

Daphne said she didn't want any dessert. She left the room quickly and clattered up the stairs faster than I'd ever heard her move before.

My mother let a spoon drop onto the table

and looked at Grandma Florence with a mixture of accusation and sadness.

"Eh-veh-lyn," Grandma Florence said innocently in a butter-smooth voice, "what did I do?" She turned to me. "Pamela and I were only whispering to ourselves. Weren't we, darling?"

Something about my mother's expression told me that I ought to leave the table, too. I finished my dessert quietly and went up to my room. Daphne's door was closed, as usual.

I tiptoed up to it and listened. There was the sound of very soft weeping coming from the TV set. Daphne's afternoon soap opera, no doubt. She seemed to love those stories. They were always about somebody's long-lost son or daughter or mother or father or wife or husband. Maybe she watched those programs and dreamed of someday finding her real, real mother. Especially now that her "adopted" mother didn't want her anymore. That probably gave her a pretty bad feeling. It meant that there were *two* sets of parents who had wanted to get rid of her.

I went to my room and fiddled around with a puzzle I was working on. In a little while, I'd get my swimming stuff together and leave for the pool as quickly as I could. But I knew my mother wouldn't let me go swimming this soon after lunch, and I figured it was better to let her calm down a little. I could still hear her and Grandma Florence having a barely polite discussion, probably about how Grandma Florence had been saying too much to me about Daphne's family problems.

On my way to the bathroom, I passed Daphne's door and stopped to listen again. The sobbing was still going on, only louder now. What a program! Fifteen minutes of crying and fourteen minutes of commercials. How could Daphne stand it? Any minute now, the swelling organ music would come on, and then the crying would end and the commercial would begin.

I tapped gently on Daphne's door. Maybe she wanted some ice cream after all.

There was no answer, so I tapped again. "Daphne," I called in a soft, raspy voice. "It's Pamela. Can I . . . come in?"

Still no answer. Only now there was no sobbing, no organ music, no commercial. There was absolute silence. No television at all. Was Daphne sleeping?

I turned the doorknob very carefully so that I wouldn't wake her up if she was. There still wasn't a sound from inside the room. So I began to push the door open as slowly as I could so as not to cause any creaking.

Now I could just see the foot of the bed. Daphne's feet were there in her socks. The bed was where she usually sat when she watched TV. Next came her knees, then the skirt of her frilly pinafore sundress that Grandma Florence had given her. Her hands were resting in her lap. There was a crumpled white hankie or tissue resting between her fingers.

Then I saw Daphne's face. She was sitting up in bed in a perfectly natural TV-watching position. Her lips wore their usual sleepy-sad smile. But her eyes looked different. They were red and puffy, so puffy that they were almost swollen shut. I realized right away that it had been Daphne I'd heard sobbing.

"Oh!" I gulped in embarrassment. "I didn't know . . . I thought I heard the TV. I figured you were . . . watching television."

"That's okay," she said in a surprisingly calm voice. "I *was* watching TV. But it was such a sad program that it actually made me cry. So I had to turn it off."

14 My mother was pretty upset. She had driven Grandma Florence to the station an hour after lunch, so she could make the afternoon train back to the city. And instead of letting me go swimming, my mother had made me go along in the car.

On the way home, she wanted to know all about what Daphne had said to me when I'd gone into her room after lunch.

"Nothing, nothing, nothing," I repeated. "She acted like nothing happened. The way she always does. Except I could tell from her eyes that she'd been crying something terrible. She said it was because of a sad program on TV. But baloney. She never even put the set on when she went upstairs. And that's something very unusual for her!"

My mother looked intently at the road.

"Pammy, we've got to do something about her. I just don't know how to help her. I feel so . . . responsible. And all I seem to get is trouble. Trouble from you, trouble from your grandmother. Oh-h-h . . ." She ground the car to a stop for a traffic light. "I have a good mind

117

not to make that bridal shower for Lainie after all. Everything I've tried to do for Daphne seems to turn out to be a disaster."

"Oh no," I clamored, in disappointment. "Don't call it off. I already promised I'd cooperate, didn't I?"

"You can have your big day at the wedding. It's only a little more than a month away. The shower would have been a little too close to the wedding anyway. And people would have had to give presents twice. . . ." My mother was rapidly talking herself out of giving the shower. "No, Pammy, my mind's made up. Daphne can meet all the relatives at the wedding. I *had* wanted to make her feel part of the family sooner, but . . ."

My mother jammed on the brakes for a stop sign.

"Wait a minute," I said, turning to her wide-eyed. "The wedding's practically in September. You don't mean to tell me that Daphne's going to be here for the *wedding!*"

My mother's eyes were fixed on the road again. "What's wrong with that?"

"Well . . . you know. September. It'll be almost time for school to begin. Doesn't she have to go back to California before then?"

"We'll see."

"What do you mean, 'we'll see'? What's there

to see? You told me she was going home at the end of the summer. I'm sure that's what you said."

"I said she was going to 'stay with us this summer,' Pammy. Don't try to pin me down to any promises or guarantees about exactly when she'll be going back. My cousin Sandra still has to get straightened out, work out some of her emotional and . . . other problems."

I screwed up my face in sheer rage.

"Oh," I exploded, writhing angrily in the front seat, "I'm beginning to see it all now. You *tricked* me. You tricked me into thinking this was all going to be temporary. Now it's beginning to seem like Daphne is going to stay with us forever! This is even worse than if you'd gone and had a baby. It's like you went and picked out a 'sister' for me. If I wanted one that badly, I'd pick one out myself!"

"Pamela, I'm driving, and you're going to make me have an accident. Quit it." My mother's voice was shrill, almost hysterical. "Quit it this instant!"

I fell back against the seat, sullen and disgusted. If my mother and father really did turn out to be Daphne's *third* set of parents, how was I going to stand having Daphne around for the rest of my life? I folded my arms and stared straight ahead of me as the car swerved recklessly into our driveway. The engine stopped, and from the open window above, which was Daphne's room, I could hear the faint sound of a television commercial.

All I could think of was Lainie's wedding at the end of the summer that I was looking forward to with all my heart. And the rotten news that Daphne was actually going to *be* here for Lainie's wedding!

It was the next morning, and I was on my way to Shirley Brummage's apartment to see how she was feeling. I was absolutely not going to ask Daphne to come along. As soon as Shirley saw her, she'd probably start all that sweet talk. And I was fed up with everybody being so sweet to Daphne—Grandma Florence, my mother and father, Shirley Brummage, even the cop in the park when we'd found her sleeping under the tree.

And did Daphne even care about Shirley Brummage? No. But just to be fair, and not get my mother any angrier than she already was, I decided I'd mention to Daphne where I was going.

"Oh," she said, looking up from a TV magazine that she was studying in her room. "Is that where you went yesterday?"

"Um hmmm," I said, not bothering to give

her any details about the flea market. "I have to
see if Shirley's leg woke up. It fell asleep yesterday around lunchtime. She had to use an
umbrella to lean on for walking, and she decided to go to bed for the rest of the afternoon."

Daphne stared. "Oh," she said, after a moment. "Well, say hello to her."

"Oh sure," I replied, deciding I wouldn't
even mention Daphne unless Shirley did.

Just as I expected, my mother made a fuss
when I left the house.

"Why *can't* you take her along?" she hissed,
as I was about to bound out the back door. "For
heaven's sake, Pamela, let's try to do *something*
to take her mind off her worries and the awful
sense of rejection she must feel. Her father
keeps sending money for her expenses, but he
never calls, and Sandra hasn't even phoned her
once this week. And when she does it's never
any good. . . ."

"Mom," I tried to explain patiently, "she
doesn't *want* to come. I told you a hundred
times my friends aren't the . . . the right age for
her. Anyhow, she has television to take her
mind off her worries. That's what she likes
best." I figured if Daphne was going to stay
with us forever, the best policy for me was to
leave her alone as much as possible. If only my
mother could also get it through her head that

that was the sensible thing to do. . . .

My mother just threw up her hands in disgust. "Okay, Pamela, go on as you're going. You want everything your way. You won't even try to help."

I made a face and growled at her. "There isn't anything I can d-o-o-o!"

I rushed off before she had a chance to say another word. Shirley had probably been up and out for a couple of hours already, and I wouldn't even know where to look for her today.

When I got to her apartment the door was locked, and although I rang the bell over and over, there was no answer. I thought of trying to peek through the sidewalk-level windows at the front of the building. But there were curtains on them in addition to the bars, and I couldn't see a thing.

I went back to the door of the apartment in the little below-ground passageway. And just as I approached it, I heard the click of a lock.

I pounded on the door. "Shirley," I called out real loud. "It's me, Pamela . . . uh, Pieface. How's your leg today? Can I come in?"

"Door's open," a voice said faintly from inside. "C'mon in."

I turned the knob and pushed open the heavy door. It was dim, almost dark in the apartment.

Why hadn't Shirley turned on any lights?

"Where are you?" I asked, groping my way across the kitchen.

"Right here," a voice said close by me. "Here in the kitchen. Git that pull chain for the ceiling light, will ya? I can't."

I found the chain and pulled it, and the room became harshly bright. I looked around, and there was Shirley, blinking hard with those cat-like green eyes. She was sitting like a limp rag doll in the easy chair in front of the TV set.

"Oh," I said, trying to conceal my shock at finding her there and looking so strangely crumpled up. "How come you're sitting here?" The TV set wasn't turned on. "How come you didn't put the light on? I didn't even think you were home. Did your leg wake up?"

"You ask too many questions, Pieface." She leaned her head against the back of the chair. "I'm just feelin' a little tired. Guess I won't be going out today."

I pulled up a little straight-backed chair and sat down opposite her.

"Well, how's your leg, anyway?"

She nodded. I couldn't tell if she meant it was better or the same.

"Well, how come you couldn't put on the light?"

Shirley grinned. "Nothin' to lean on. Had to

hold onto the cane with my right hand. Guess my left arm fell asleep, too. Dang stupid thing, ain't it?"

I leaned forward.

"You mean your left arm *and* your left leg fell asleep?"

"Yeah. I guess so." She made a jabbing motion at me with her right arm. "But it ain't nothin', Pieface. I got all the way over to the door, didn't I? Got the door unlocked. Got myself outa bed this A.M. That's something. Nope, I ain't down yet."

I scratched my head. "Well, how long do you figure this might go on? I mean, shouldn't your leg have woken up by now? It's kind of inconvenient, isn't it, having both your leg *and* arm asleep at the same time?"

"Yeah," she admitted, "pretty inconvenient."

I glanced around the kitchen. Everything was just as it had been the day before. There was no sign of any food or cooking. "Hey," I remarked, "I bet you didn't even have anything to eat. On account of it being so hard to get around."

"Aw, I had some stuff outa the fridge." Shirley sighed. "I'm okay. Don't need nothin' from nobody. Another day or two, I'll be up and around." She paused, her eyes glittering. "Tell you one thing I could use, though. I could use a cup of hot coffee. Yeah, that'd be real nice."

I looked around helplessly. "I don't really know how to make coffee, Shirley. But listen, I could run over to the luncheonette at the corner and get you a container to take out. And . . . and maybe a sandwich or some toast or something like that, huh?"

Shirley's head was nodding to one side. Was she saying yes or was she falling asleep?

"Stay right where you are," I said. "I'll be back in a jiffy. I won't even lock the door. So you won't have to get up to let me in when I get back. Okay?"

Shirley's head had stopped nodding. It hung to one side against the back of the chair. It wasn't surprising that with the whole left side of her body asleep her head had gone to sleep also. Once she smelled the hot coffee, though, she'd probably sit up straight and rub her hands together the way my father did every morning.

I tiptoed away from Shirley very quietly so as not to wake her. Then I checked the door to make sure it would stay unlocked after I closed it, and I carefully let myself out of the apartment.

15 The luncheonette down the street from Shirley's building was crowded with late-morning customers. I shifted from one foot to the other until I got the woman behind the counter to take my order.

"One coffee to go," she repeated. "Milk? Sugar?"

How should I know?

"Yes," I decided quickly, "stick 'em all in."

I could see it would take forever to get a sandwich made up or even some hot toast. So I told the woman to put two doughnuts into the bag. I was sure Shirley would like those.

I hurried back toward the apartment, hoping the coffee wouldn't get cold.

As I was about to turn into the sloping walkway that led down to Shirley's door, I saw a familiar figure coming toward me on the street. I stopped short. I couldn't believe my eyes. It was Daphne.

"What are *you* doing here?" I asked her coldly.

"I got to wondering," she said calmly. "How's Shirley?"

"She's fine," I replied, trying to brush past her quickly. "Just fine. I went out to get her some hot coffee. She said that was what she felt like the most. I have to hurry. She's waiting for it."

"Can I come with you?"

"What for?" I asked suspiciously.

"Oh, just to see her."

"She really isn't in the mood for company. In fact, she told me she didn't want to see anybody today," I lied.

I noticed that Daphne was following me down the walkway to the apartment anyhow. What nerve! Shirley was *my* friend. I didn't want Daphne poking her nose in. If she did, Shirley might forget all about what I was doing for her and start admiring Daphne, who wasn't doing *anything*. What had she followed me here for, anyway?

I put my hand on the doorknob and I could feel Daphne practically breathing down my back.

"You wait outside," I ordered her. "I have to see what she says. She might be asleep."

"But I thought you said she wanted coffee."

"She does."

I let the door slam shut in Daphne's face. It served her right. Did she think she could walk in here anytime she felt like it just because there wasn't anything she wanted to watch on television that morning?

I put the coffee and doughnuts on the kitchen table. Shirley hadn't changed her position at all since I'd left. I guessed she'd probably had a restless night trying to wake up her arm and her leg, and now she was tired.

"Shirley," I said, leaning over her, "I brought you some nice hot coffee. And doughnuts. Fat, puffy ones. Why don't you wake up?"

But Shirley seemed dead to the world. She was so fast asleep that her mouth was open and her tongue was lolling in one corner of it.

I heard a sound and I jumped. The doorknob was turning very, very slowly. After a moment, the door opened a crack and Daphne peeked in. I could see it wasn't going to be easy to get rid of her.

"She's sleeping," I hissed across the room. "All right, all right. If you *have* to come in, you can. Maybe you can help me wake her up and get her to drink her coffee."

Daphne walked softly over to Shirley's easy chair where I was standing. She looked down at Shirley, and then she looked up at me with pained eyes.

"Pamela, you have to call somebody. She's sick."

"Oh, what are you talking about?" All of a

sudden Daphne was getting to be a real know-it-all. "She's fine. She was talking to me just a little while ago."

Daphne shook her head. "She doesn't look . . . right."

I put my head to one side, trying to line it up with Shirley's. Her face did look odd. "Well, she's just very sound asleep," I explained to Daphne. "It's too bad, because now her coffee's going to get cold."

Daphne was still shaking her head. "Can't you see how funny she's sitting, all keeled over? Her entire body's . . . collapsed, sort of."

"Oh," I said, "that's only because her left arm fell asleep, too. Her left arm and leg are both asleep since last night. Or maybe early this morning."

"That's what it is, then!" Daphne exclaimed. She turned and started for the door.

"Where are you going?"

"To find a—a policeman. Or somebody."

I ran over and grabbed her arm. "Why?"

"To get an ambulance. To take her to the hospital. She's sick, Pamela."

"How do you know?" I challenged. "Are you a doctor or something?"

"Uh-uh," Daphne said stubbornly. "But I know. A person shouldn't look like that if they're just sleeping. It happened once to a

129

next-door neighbor who used to take care of me sometimes when I was younger. It's called a stroke. Something happens to your brain and part of you gets paralyzed."

Brain! Paralyzed! I couldn't believe it.

"There is nothing wrong with Shirley's brain," I shouted at Daphne. "And she is *not* paralyzed."

I turned to glance at Shirley. In spite of my speaking so loudly, she hadn't stirred.

Daphne wrenched her arm away from me. Her cheeks were darkly flushed. "You'd better stop yelling, Pamela," she retorted. "I'm older than you and . . . and you have to listen to me."

I couldn't believe that Daphne was actually talking to me this way. I had a feeling that she couldn't believe it, either. Maybe something serious really was happening to Shirley. Deep down, I was beginning to get awfully trembly and scared.

Daphne reached for the doorknob. "I knew something was wrong when you told me this morning that her leg had fallen asleep yesterday and she couldn't walk. So she *has* to go to the hospital. It might even be too late already."

The door slammed shut behind Daphne. I stood there stunned, and then I turned to Shirley. I still couldn't believe—didn't *want* to believe—there was anything wrong with her.

"C'mon, Shirley," I begged. "Wake up and drink your coffee." I glanced toward the door through which Daphne had vanished. "What do you want to listen to Daphne for? She's full of prunes."

I hated for it to be true, but Daphne turned out to be right after all, and everyone agreed that she'd done a heroic deed by being so quick-witted in getting help for Shirley. Maybe she had even saved Shirley's life.

"Everyone"—so far—was my mother, the ambulance attendant, the admitting doctor at the hospital, and Mrs. Ramirez, the wife of the superintendent of the building where Shirley lived.

When Daphne had left Shirley's apartment, she had looked around in the street for a policeman. But there wasn't any in sight. Then she ran into the main entrance of the apartment building and rang the superintendent's bell. And Mrs. Ramirez had phoned the emergency number for an ambulance. Shirley, of course, didn't have a telephone in her apartment.

Later, after Mrs. Ramirez had gone off in the ambulance with Shirley, and Daphne and I had gone home and gotten my astonished and confused mother to drive us to the hospital, we all met in the hospital lobby.

"You got a wonderful little girl here, missus," Mrs. Ramirez assured my mother. She had her arm wrapped affectionately around Daphne's shoulders. "An angel. An angel of mercy. That Brummage lady, I'm telling you, she was a strange one. Always to herself, you know. Not easy to talk to. Close-mouthed. Paid her rent on time, and that was that. I didn't think the lady had a friend in the world. And now this sweet, beautiful child turns up. I'm telling you, like an angel . . ."

Of course, Daphne did deserve full credit for deciding that Shirley had to go to the hospital. But that was only because she was older and had more experience. How was *I* supposed to know the difference between a leg that had fallen asleep and one that had gotten paralyzed? And why was my mother letting Mrs. Ramirez think that Daphne was her "little girl"? Why didn't she explain?

I tugged hard on my mother's arm. "What about Shirley, huh? Can I see her? Find out."

Mrs. Ramirez looked at me and shook her head. "Oh no, they won't let anybody up to see her. Especially not a little kid like you."

"Oh no?" I barked. "I happen to be her best friend."

Just then, a woman at the reception desk called out Shirley's name, and we all rushed over to talk to a young doctor in a wrinkled white coat who was supposed to tell us how she was.

"She's had a rapid series of moderately severe strokes," he said. "Paralysis of the left side. Her speech may be slightly impaired as well. We can't tell the full extent of the damage yet."

Daphne sent me a knowing look. Okay, okay, I admitted. I guess you were right. But the person I really cared about right now was Shirley.

"Will she die?" I demanded. "Or is she going to get better?"

The young doctor looked at me with faint annoyance.

"Is this her granddaughter?"

"No, no," my mother said quickly. "We're . . . friends. She doesn't seem to have any family. Uh, that we know of. Please go on."

"Well," he said, "right now her condition seems to have stabilized. She's resting comfortably. That's all I can tell you."

"When can we come to see her?" I asked.

He answered without even looking at me. "No visitors yet," he said coldly. "We'll let you know."

At home, I went straight to my room and shut the door. I felt as though a steel gate had clanged shut between Shirley Brummage and me. Even if she didn't die, she seemed to have changed into somebody else. She wasn't the snappy, fresh-talking Shirley I'd known. She was a sick old woman with a crooked face and a lolling tongue. She didn't even know who I was.

I tried not thinking about the terrible thing that had happened. I moped around in my room. I stared at a puzzle I'd been working on, and suddenly it didn't seem interesting anymore. I opened and shut a couple of books I'd been planning to read. Then I sat down on the edge of my bed, and a big tear fell—plop—on my knee.

I don't know how long I sat there, tears like big raindrops falling into my lap. All of a sudden, my mother was crouching in front of me. She put a finger under my chin.

"Pammy, Pammy, what a funny kid you are. You never even told me about your friend. Why? Did you think I'd be angry? I'd have been delighted to know you were befriending a poor old woman, helping her collect trash and stuff to eke out some sort of livelihood—"

"I wasn't," I interrupted her, between sobs. "It wasn't like that. Shirley isn't . . . wasn't . . . a poor old woman. She was tough and . . . sassy. She always got her own way about things." I choked and gulped hard. "She would never even c-c-call me by my real name. She always called me . . . Pieface. But I liked her. We got along fine. She was more fun than any of the kids I know. And more interesting."

"I'm sure she was . . . is," my mother said comfortingly. "It sounds like an unusual but very nice relationship. I'm sure she'll get better and be her old self again."

I shook my head miserably. "You don't have to soft-soap me. She won't." I lifted my head and looked straight at my mother. "And, anyhow, I'm mad at you."

My mother drew back in surprise. "Why?"

"You should know why. Why didn't you tell that dumb Mrs. Ramirez that Daphne wasn't your 'little girl'? Why did you let her think she was?"

My mother took a deep breath and sat down on the bed next to me. "Pamela, was that so important? Couldn't you be big enough to let it pass? Daphne's been disowned so many times already. Today was a big day for her, a sort of turning point in which she came out of herself and did something really . . . meaningful. I didn't want to spoil it for her."

"Daphne, Daphne," I groaned. "It's always Daphne!"

My mother jumped up almost angrily.

"Pamela, you're shameless. Why shouldn't it be Daphne's turn to shine? She hasn't had the love and advantages you have. She's had a truly messed-up life. You should be glad that she had the chance to do what she did for Shirley. But, if it makes you feel any better, you can take a lot of the credit for what happened today, too."

I looked up at her through tear-blurred eyes.

"Yes," she said emphatically. "In an indirect way, you helped both of them, Shirley *and* Daphne."

I shook my head, too unhappy and confused to understand.

"Don't you see? If not for your having made a friendship with Shirley, Daphne would have spent today sitting in front of the television screen, as usual. And Shirley might possibly have died alone in her apartment."

My mother paused, eyeing me carefully. "Now do you see what I mean? Think about it."

16 Daphne got to meet my grown-up cousin Lainie before the wedding after all. The way it happened was that my mother and Daphne and I went to the bridal shop where Lainie was having a fitting of her wedding dress and where I was supposed to pick out my flower girl's outfit.

The wedding was only a few weeks off now, and Daphne and I had been spending a lot more time together because I'd decided that we should keep up Shirley Brummage's "business" while she was in the hospital, slowly learning to use her left arm and leg again. So, a couple of days each week, we went scouting around the neighborhood for the kind of trash I knew Shirley usually picked out, and we also took stuff to the recycling plant and put the money aside for Shirley.

I couldn't do anything about cashing in the coupons, though. My father said it was against the law for a storeowner or supermarket manager to "buy" them from Shirley in batches the way it had appeared. "He was probably just taking them off her hands and not even cashing them in, just giving her a few dollars from time to time to help her out," my father explained. "She must have known the truth. But she didn't want to admit even to herself that she was taking charity. That was why she was being so hush-hush about what she was doing with those coupons."

"Hush-hush" really was the word for poor Shirley now that she wasn't able to talk very well. But my mother phoned the hospital a couple of times each week, and they always said Shirley was "showing improvement." So I was hoping to be able to visit her one of these days, as soon as she was well enough to have company. Meantime, the old Shirley seemed almost to be trudging along with Daphne and me on the days we went out collecting junk. We even used Shirley's wagon, which Mrs. Ramirez had given us from Shirley's apartment.

The bridal shop where we were supposed to meet Lainie was called Paulette's Bridal Boutique. It was like a winter fairyland inside, with its displays of snowy veils and frosty white satin. Daphne just loved it and went around touching and stroking the wedding outfits on the mannequins.

After a while, Lainie came bursting out of one of the dressing rooms, kissed us all, and exclaimed over how glad she was to meet Daphne at last, because she'd heard so much about her from Grandma Florence. Lainie was wearing a beautiful white lace and organdy dress that fell in rich tiers all the way to the ground. She stood on tiptoes because she was wearing tennis shoes and didn't want the hem of her wedding dress to get dirty.

"What do you think, Aunt Evelyn?" She twirled around in front of my mother. "Wait till you see the veil. They're trimming it just a tiny bit shorter. It was too long and we decided it took something away from the dress."

Lainie cupped my face between her slender fingers and gently squeezed my cheeks. "Pamela, your dress will be a sort of copy of mine, with tiers of organdy and lace. It's aw-fully expensive but—guess what—Grandma Florence is going to pay for it. She says she wants you to have the 'very best.' "

I beamed at my mother and glanced over at Daphne. Daphne was standing very still in front of one of the bridal dresses that was on display, her mouth solemn and her eyes fastened to the figure before her.

A big-boned woman with tightly curled red hair came out of the fitting room carrying Lainie's veil in her two hands like a freshly iced cake.

"Ah," she said, "I see the little flower girl is here. I'll bring out the dress in a moment."

Soon we all went into one of the bigger try-on rooms and everybody watched as the red-haired woman, who turned out to be Paulette herself, carefully slipped the flower girl's dress on over my head and began fastening the tiny buttons down the back.

"Too big," she muttered through a mouthful of pins. "I don't have the smaller size in the shop right now, but we'll get an idea anyway. Hold still, doll."

I could feel her pulling and tugging at the back of the dress. My mother and Daphne and Lainie stood watching. I smiled. "How does it look?"

Everybody seemed to be concentrating on what Paulette was doing to the dress. My mother wore a very slight frown.

"Don't worry, ladies," Paulette mumbled through pins. "This dress can't miss. It's a stunner. You'll see."

After a while, she gave me a little push. "Okay, doll, walk over to the mirror. But slow. Don't trip. In this size, it's *much* too long for you."

Holding the skirt up daintily, I took very small steps and walked past everyone to the big full-length mirror.

140

The first thing I saw in the glass was my face, my hair framing it, black and smooth and shiny, my eyes full of happy expectation. I smiled, thinking how Shirley had explained why she called me Pieface. My face *was* round, and maybe it wasn't as pretty as Daphne's. But it was pretty enough, especially when I was wearing a dress as fantastic as this.

Then I looked down at the reflection of the dress itself, and all of a sudden my insides seemed to go . . . *flump!* I looked over at Lainie's dress, which she still had on, and then back at my dress. The two *were* almost exactly alike. Yet Lainie's dress looked beautiful on her because she was tall and willowy, while mine looked, well . . . potty.

Mountains of frilly lace and puffy organdy were engulfing me from all sides. There were layers of ruffles at the neck, and short frilly sleeves. I looked almost as wide as I was high. Paulette came up from behind and stuck a wreath of white flowers and veiling on top of my head. Now I looked just like a round, squat, white teapot—with the lid on!

I turned to my mother disappointedly.

"I don't know," I said. "It's so . . . ruffly and frilly. I don't think it's the right style for me."

"It's for a *wedding*," Paulette exclaimed before my mother could say anything. "The child looks delectable in it. Like a piece of cake. What should she wear for such an occasion? A baseball outfit?"

"Perhaps," my mother began hesitantly, "if you had something simpler, with a straighter line . . . a high waist, let's say, and a plain skirt. No tiers. . . ."

Paulette shook her head. "I beg to differ, my dear. It wouldn't look in keeping with the bride's gown. You have to see the bridal procession as a whole unit. Know what I mean?" She came up behind me again and bunched the dress together tighter at the back with her hands. "You'll see the difference when I get it for you in the right size."

As Paulette squinted into the mirror to examine my reflection, her glance suddenly lighted on Daphne's image reflected in the glass. She turned quickly.

"Here, I'll show you what I mean. Let me borrow this angel-faced little beauty for a minute. The dress is her size exactly." She beckoned to Daphne. "Please. If you don't mind."

Lainie gently pushed Daphne forward. "Go ahead," she whispered. "Try it on."

Daphne looked around her perplexed.

"Come on, doll. Don't be shy." Paulette began to unpin and unbutton me with nimble fingers. "The right size makes *all* the difference," she said, lifting the billowy dress up over my head.

In a few minutes the dress was on Daphne instead. Paulette did up the last button and said, "There!" Daphne was only a little taller and a little thinner than I, but her pretty face and softly curling hair were just right for all those frills and lace. Instead of looking like a fat, foolish clown in the flower girl's dress, she looked like a fairy princess.

Paulette knelt down and fussed with the skirt, telling Daphne what an "absolutely stunning little model" she was. Then she carefully placed the wreath of flowers on Daphne's head.

Everybody said, "A-h-h-h," and Paulette went and leaned against the doorway of the fitting room, smiling with satisfaction.

"Convinced, ladies?"

Daphne studied herself in the mirror. She walked right up to the glass and actually touched it carefully, as if she expected it might shatter. Then she slowly turned around and around.

Paulette directed her attention to me. "And that," she said with emphasis, "is *exactly* how the flower girl's outfit should look on you."

I gave her a sour look.

"It *should*," I thought disgustedly, "but it won't."

After Paulette took my exact measurements for the smaller-size dress and we all changed back to our regular clothes, Lainie dashed off to meet Elliot, her fiancé, and my mother and Daphne and I drove to Grandma Florence's apartment, where we had been invited for lunch.

Grandma Florence looked even younger and healthier than the last time I'd seen her. She had bright lipstick on and her apartment was filled with vases of fresh flowers. As usual, she and my mother had gotten back on friendly terms again. Grandma Florence never let anybody stay mad at her for long, no matter what she'd done to get them angry in the first place.

"So," she said, bustling around the table, which was all set up for a fancy cold lunch, "how did the fitting go? Isn't that some terrific dress I picked out for you, Pamela darling?"

"It's kind of . . . fussy," I replied haltingly. "It looked a lot better on Daphne. Why do you want to spend so much money on me, anyway?"

Grandma Florence smiled. "Why not? For *my* grandchildren, nothing but the best."

"Pamela does look better in simpler styles," my mother pointed out gently. "I wonder if it's really so important that the flower girl's dress should match the bride's—"

"I thought *I* was supposed to pick out my

own outfit," I interrupted. "But when we got there, this lady said that was what I *had* to wear. How come?"

"Let's eat," Grandma Florence said. "We'll talk later. Here, Daphne darling, you sit on one side of me. Pamela sweetie, you sit on the other side of Grandma."

She looked back and forth admiringly at both of us. Her glance finally lighted on Daphne. "I feel like I just added a brand-new grandchild to my batch of beautiful grandchildren."

Daphne smiled shyly.

Grandma Florence turned to my mother. "Isn't that wedding dress of Lainie's something, Evelyn? She looks like a million dollars in it, no?"

My mother dug into her chicken salad. "I thought it was going to be a small, rather modest wedding. Looks to me like it's turning out to be a big, splashy, expensive affair."

Grandma Florence shrugged. "So, it's growing. Is there some law against that? I like to see things done up nice, Evelyn. And I don't mind paying for some of the extras. After all, how do I know I'll be around the next time one of my grandchildren gets married?"

My mother looked up with a funny little smile on her face. "Oh, Ma, you will. You will."

But Grandma Florence wasn't listening. She

was leaning over and talking to Daphne. "What was that I heard Pamela say? You tried on the dress?"

Daphne flushed slightly. "Just for the size. They have to order a smaller size for Pamela because the one they had at the shop was too big. It was the right size for me."

Grandma Florence looked at Daphne with interest. "Really?"

"It did look better on her, too," I commented. "Ruffles are great on her. They're terrible on me." It seemed a good time to let Grandma Florence know how I felt about the clothing presents she was always bringing me. Maybe she'd finally get the message. "And," I continued, "the skirt's too full. . . ."

But Grandma Florence wasn't paying any attention to me. "It was just your size?" she was asking Daphne. "A perfect fit?"

"Um hmmm," Daphne replied politely. "Only a little too long."

"Long is nothing," Grandma Florence said. "What is there to turning up a hem? And besides, alterations are free."

I looked up from my plate in alarm and met my mother's wide-eyed stare. Was the very same thought running through both our heads at once? *Was* Grandma Florence thinking of adding Daphne to Lainie's wedding procession as flower girl number two?

Why not? With Grandma Florence, anything was possible.

17 My mother and father and I were having a secret midnight conference in my parents' bedroom. Daphne was asleep in her own room, probably with a smile on her lips.

My father was pacing up and down in his pajamas and bathrobe. He had his glasses on and was tugging at his earlobe as though he was at an important business conference in his accountancy office. My mother and I were sitting huddled together on the bed.

"Sidney," my mother was pleading,' "she's *your* mother. Please think of something. Pamela's just crushed. She's looked forward all summer to this flower girl thing. No one could be more in favor of making Daphne feel a part of our family, but even I think this is too much. Your mother's simply gone too far."

I wriggled around among the crumpled wads of wet tissue on my parents' bed. I was exhausted and giddy from tears that had started soon after I'd closed the door of my room that night. I kept seeing myself coming down the aisle in that awful, flumpy flower girl's dress, with Daphne beside me or behind me, looking meltingly beautiful and everyone saying, "A-h-h-h," barely saving their final sighs of admiration for the bride herself.

How could Grandma Florence do such a thing to me? She'd fixed it specially so that I could *be* a flower girl at Lainie's wedding, and now she'd ruined it all, first with the dress she'd ordered for me and then with her hints about Daphne's being a flower girl, too.

"But did she actually *say* she was going to order that dress for Daphne?" my father wanted to know.

"Well," my mother explained, "not in so many words. But she talked about having the hem shortened. Isn't it clear what she has in mind?"

"In that case," my father said, "it's too late already. Daphne heard her, too, and she probably already sees herself coming down the aisle at the wedding."

"Oh Sidney," my mother lamented, "this is awful. I didn't want both Pamela *and* Daphne to be hurt." She hugged me closer. "Pam's been crying her eyes out with disappointment."

My father stopped pacing and dug his hands into his bathrobe pockets.

"Please calm down, Evvie. There's no use weeping and wailing. The trouble with all you

149

do-gooders is that you never know when to stop."

My mother sat up straight. "What do you mean by that? Are you lumping your mother and me together?"

My father tugged harder at his earlobe. "In this respect, yes," he said. "You want to make the whole world happy, you want everybody to have everything. And then, when somebody gets hurt in the process, you're surprised."

My mother got to her feet with a start, so suddenly, in fact, that I rolled over and nearly fell off the bed.

"How can you say such a thing, Sidney? I'm not responsible for this problem."

My father looked up at the bedroom ceiling in despair. "I only know one thing. I'll be glad when this wedding is over. I knew from the start that it wouldn't stay small or uncomplicated. I knew it would grow, step by step, into a devouring monster. . . ."

My mother was dabbing at her eyes with a crushed tissue. "That's the cruelest and most unfair thing I ever heard you say . . . to blame me for a mixup that I had nothing to do with. . . ."

"O-h-h-h," I burst out, "don't *you* two start arguing. It's bad enough. I'm beginning to not even care anymore. I'm actually starting to hate the whole idea. Everything's turning out to be a great big . . . bomb!"

And I padded off disgustedly to my room.

It was finally arranged that I could visit Shirley Brummage in the hospital. Naturally, Daphne was coming, too. And my mother was going to drive us there.

These days, everything between Daphne and me was share and share alike, just the way my mother had always wanted it to be. And I hope she was satisfied! Sure enough, Grandma Florence had phoned Paulette and told her to hold the dress in Daphne's size. And she had easily persuaded Lainie to add a second flower girl to the wedding procession.

What could I do? I felt beaten down and cheated and horrible. Yet Daphne was so happy and pleased to get to wear that beautiful dress and to be part of the wedding that I didn't have the heart to be mean to her about it. My mother said I was being "mature and sensible." But inside, I was really hurting.

Did my mother think I could change overnight? It wasn't easy to give up all my dreams about how I'd look coming down the aisle, the only child in the wedding ceremony. Daphne wasn't even an *adopted* relative of Lainie's. She was from the opposite side of the family. Yet we all had to be extra nice to her. The only good thing was that the summer was coming to an end. Any day now, my mother and Daphne's mother, Sandra, would have to get together on the phone and decide on a date for Daphne to return to California in time for the opening of school.

Meantime, of course, I had to share Shirley Brummage with Daphne, too. At the hospital, my mother and Daphne and I all went up in the elevator together and sort of tiptoed down the long corridor until we came to the number of the room they'd told us Shirley was in.

My mother hung back. "I think you two should go in first," she whispered. "She doesn't know me, and anyhow we shouldn't all descend on a sick person at once." She gave us each a little send-off pat on the back and I started toward Shirley's doorway.

To my surprise, Daphne remained standing where she was. I had been getting so used to doing things with her, whether I wanted to or not, that I suddenly felt as though I'd lost my shadow. And maybe I did want Daphne beside me just this once. It felt odd coming to see Shirley in a strange place like this, and I had no idea what to expect when I got inside that hospital room.

"Aren't you coming?"

Daphne made a little gesture with her hand. "I will. But why don't you go on in first, Pamela?"

"Oh," I said, "how come? You're the one who practically saved her life. Maybe you should be the one to go in first?"

Doubt flickered in Daphne's violet eyes. "Uh, no. That's not what I was thinking." She looked uncomfortably from me to my mother. "It's really that Pamela was Shirley's friend first, and I thought she . . . she should be the first one to see her now that she's better."

Daphne looked into my eyes with a clear gaze. "I'll go with you if you really want me to. It's just that I didn't want to . . . well, get in your way." She glanced down at the floor. "I think I do. A lot."

I felt strangely choked up. I looked at my mother, and she nodded and smiled. It did seem hard to walk into Shirley's hospital room alone. And yet it was exactly what I wanted to do. How had Daphne been wise enough to know that?

G-u-u-l-p. I swallowed a very large lump in my throat and marched through the doorway. There were two beds. The first one had a ceiling-to-floor white curtain drawn partway around it. In the second bed, over near the window, sat Shirley Brummage, propped up against the pillows and looking surprisingly fresh and perky. She had a lavender velvet ribbon tied around her gray-white hair, and the ribbon was knotted into a pretty bow that tilted over one eye.

"Well," she exclaimed, sounding almost exactly like her old self, "if it ain't Pieface."

"Wow," I said, grinning. "You really are all better."

"Oh yeah," she said. "Except for *that* dang thing." She pointed to a rubber and metal contraption with crossbars and handles that stood beside the bed. It looked something like a supermarket shopping cart without the basket part and with rubber-coated feet instead of wheels.

"What's *that?*"

"It's called a walker, m'dear. Got to march around with that for a partner every time I git outa bed. Keeps me from stumblin' and crashin'."

"Oh, I see. You mean in case your leg gets . . . paralyzed again."

"I mean *until* my leg gets totally *un*-paralyzed," Shirley corrected. She leaned farther back against the pillows with a sigh. "Yeah, it'll be a while yet till I git to go out on my rounds again, Pieface. Guess my junk business has been goin' all to pot these last weeks."

154

"No it ain't—isn't," I told her. "You see, Daphne and me—I—that is, well we're collecting junk for you. We've got all sorts of things out in the shed in my backyard. And you can come look them over when you get out of here. And," I continued, "we've also got some money put aside for you from stuff we've been taking to the recycling plant. Daphne and I go there once a week."

I paused. I hoped the mention of the money hadn't been a mistake. Of course, I wasn't going to say anything at all about the coupons. After what my father had told me about how the money Shirley got for the ones she cut out was really charity in disguise, I had stopped collecting them. The last thing I wanted to do was to hurt Shirley's pride.

Shirley looked as though she was pleased that Daphne and I were keeping up the junk business. But she didn't say anything. I wondered why she had gotten so quiet. I had thought that surely the mention of Daphne's name, if nothing else, would get a rise out of her. Finally I decided to come straight out with it and tell her that Daphne was waiting to see her.

"Guess what?" I said brightly. "Daphne's here, too. She's waiting outside because she thought I should see you first."

155

Shirley smiled wanly. Maybe she was getting tired. She wasn't completely well yet, after all.

"Pieface and Daphne," she muttered almost dreamily. "Yeah, that's really a double bonus. I'd a settled for Pieface alone."

Shirley closed her eyes. But she went on talking, almost as if to herself. "Still, I guess what they say is true. Ya can't have too many friends. Never know when you might need 'em."

She began to blink rapidly. Her head had begun to slump downward on the pillows and her voice was growing fainter. "Yeah, sure. I'd like to see Daphne, too. Mebbe next time. You know, when I got more strength."

I looked at Shirley in alarm, and just then a nurse in a crinkly white pants suit came into the room and moved swiftly toward Shirley's bed. She lifted Shirley's limp wrist. By now, Shirley's eyes had completely closed again and she appeared to be asleep.

After a few moments of holding Shirley's wrist, the nurse looked at me and smiled. "You must be Pieface."

I was shocked. "How did you know?"

"Oh, she talks about you a lot. She told me you were coming today. She says you're her best friend. Did you have a good visit with her?"

I nodded, still perplexed at the way Shirley

156

had just sort of faded out before I had a chance to call Daphne in.

The nurse released Shirley's wrist and gently placed it on the bedcover.

"Don't worry," she said, studying my face. "She drops off this way quite a lot. She's still pretty feeble. That's why short visits are best. She'll be okay."

"Do you really think so?"

"Oh sure," she answered quickly. "All she needs right now is forty winks."

I left the room slowly, still puzzled. I couldn't help glowing over what the nurse said Shirley had told her, about my being her *best* friend, and remembering that Shirley hadn't asked for Daphne even at the start, when she'd been wide awake and talkative.

So maybe I'd been wrong after all in thinking that Shirley Brummage liked Daphne better than me. But, of course, I wouldn't tell that to Daphne.

18 It was exactly one week before Lainie's wedding and we had just had a rehearsal in the empty chapel, with Grandma Florence and a strange, silver-haired man who played the organ, and Lainie and Elliot, and both their sets of parents, and the maid of honor, who was Lainie's best friend, and the best man, who was Elliot's best friend, and four bridesmaids, and Daphne and me. As my father said, the wedding *had* become a devouring monster that was steadily eating up more and more people and money and clothing . . . and food.

There was this big problem about scattering the rose petals out of our baskets in the procession. If I walked in front of Daphne and scattered them, that meant Daphne would be walking on them before Lainie, the bride, and that wasn't right. So it was finally decided that Daphne and I would walk side by side, being careful not to scatter too *many* rose petals and especially careful not to bump baskets.

After the rehearsal, Grandma Florence brought over the silver-haired man and introduced him to everybody as Herman. She kept her arm through his the whole time. It turned out he wasn't really an organist but a friend of Grandma Florence's who happened to play the organ.

"What do you think of my two adorable flower girls, Herman?" Grandma Florence asked him. "Maybe you'd be interested in hiring them for a future occasion?" Grandma Florence looked up at Herman and winked. Then she squeezed his wrist hard with her other hand.

Everybody broke out in little murmurs of suspicion and approval. "Grandma!" Lainie shrieked. "Are you talking about wedding bells?"

"Sssh. Sssh," Grandma Florence commanded, with her finger on her lips. "We're only talking about one wedding at a time in this family. I wouldn't dream of stealing your thunder, my darling."

Herman, meantime, had stood beside Grandma Florence smiling and grunting warmly. He was portly and suntanned and had very large white teeth. He was a little taller than Grandpa Morris had been and he had more hair and didn't wear glasses. But he seemed just right for Grandma Florence. No wonder she'd been wearing so much makeup lately and had so many vases of flowers all over her apartment.

On the way home from the rehearsal, I had a million questions to ask my parents. "Do you really think she's going to marry him? When? How come he's so suntanned? Does that mean I get to be a flower girl again?"

My father, who was driving the car "recklessly," according to my mother, answered me jauntily. "How should I know? I'm only her son."

My mother laughed. "Come on, Sidney. You suspected it."

The only other thing I managed to find out was that Herman lived in Florida all year and that was why he was so suntanned.

"Does that mean that if Grandma Florence marries him, she'll be moving permanently to . . ."

My mother turned around in the front seat and nodded.

"Wow," I exclaimed, "that'd be—"

My mother placed a finger of caution on her lips.

"Great for *her!*" I blurted. "I mean, she could also be suntanned all year round."

Daphne, who was sitting beside me in the backseat, looked at me and smiled faintly.

Two days later, my mother drove us to

160

Paulette's Bridal Boutique for our final fittings. Daphne's dress had only had to be shortened. But mine still had to be tried on in the smaller size that Paulette had ordered.

Paulette came hurrying out of her office when she saw us enter the bridal shop. Her thin, plucked eyebrows were drawn into two long, dark, angry lines across her olive skin.

"Ladies," she said, rubbing her hands together as if she had just come in from the cold, "I've just had terrible news."

We all looked at her in alarm.

"Never, never, never," she swore, rolling her eyes toward the ceiling, "will I deal with that supplier again. They promised me faithfully to have number FG 3146 here yesterday morning. It didn't arrive. I phoned them again this morning. I told them, 'Today is Tuesday.' I told them, 'The wedding is Sunday.' I told them there would probably be a few alterations. I said, 'What am I going to tell the customer?' "

A large, mascara-darkened tear actually rolled down Paulette's cheek.

My mother touched her arm. "What are you saying? You haven't got the dress?"

Paulette dabbed at her blackened cheek with a lace-edged hankie. "That's what I'm saying. I haven't got the dress in the smaller size for your little girl. I've got the other one, the bigger size." She turned to Daphne. "That one's all ready. You can take it home with you today."

I looked up at Paulette in horror. "But what about me? What am I going to wear?"

Paulette spread her hands. "There is . . . one thing I can suggest. . . ."

To my surprise, Daphne didn't let her finish. "I know what," she interrupted, "you—you can still make my dress smaller to fit *her*. You can do that, can't you?" Daphne's face was flushed and her eyes were unnaturally bright.

Paulette shrugged. "Sure. It's a possibility. What do I care? I'll do anything not to disappoint a customer. I'll remake the entire dress. I'll sit up all night. You think it's easy to build up a business? Can I afford to let my reputation go to pieces . . . ?"

Paulette suddenly stopped herself. "But what are we talking about? That's no good. What will *you* wear? I can't get *any* other FG 3146's. Not in *any* size. The model is discontinued. That's what they finally told me. Didn't I explain about that?"

"No, you don't understand," Daphne said, backing away. "*I* won't be a flower girl at all. I never should have been in the first place. I'm not even . . . related."

162

"Wait a minute," my mother said. "This is all nonsense. Daphne's dress is ready and there's no reason she shouldn't wear it as planned. Surely there must be something else we can pick out for Pamela in her size."

Paulette looked doubtful. "Right now I have only one number in stock. I'm not sure you'd like it. It's very plain. It's off-white instead of pure white. It's a satin-finish polyester instead of organdy. No lace, no tiers. It wouldn't match the other outfits. The older lady, the one who's ordering—the grandmother, I believe—I'm afraid she wouldn't like it at all."

Paulette tucked her stained hankie into her sleeve, shook her red-dyed curls, and went on talking.

"Now, of course, *if* the older lady wouldn't mind the expense, I could send you to a dressmaker and you could have the original flower girl's dress duplicated, in the smaller size. It would be a rush job so it would cost a little extra, you understand. Well, quite a bit extra. But it would be a very good copy. And I'd guarantee it would fit the smaller girl perfectly. After all, a wedding is a once-in-a-lifetime experience. You don't want to spoil it. Could you ever forgive yourself?"

My mother bit her lip in uncertainty. "I just

163

can't see putting my mother-in-law to so much additional expense," she murmured, "and it would be such a last-minute rush."

"It could be done," Paulette urged. "Why don't we call the . . . the older Mrs. Teitelbaum and ask her? Come on, the phone's in my office."

"No!" I declared in such a loud voice that Paulette stopped in her tracks. "I want to try on the other dress. The one that doesn't match."

Paulette looked dismayed. "You're sure?" She tugged at a red curl. "Well, maybe you ladies should convince yourselves. Seeing is believing, they say."

Ten minutes later, I was parading up and down in front of the mirror in the big dressing room.

"I like it," I said. "I really, really like it."

The dress had a simple round neckline, short not-too-puffy sleeves, and a high waist. From the waistline to the floor it was perfectly straight and slender-looking.

"Now wait. Be fair to yourselves," Paulette warned my mother. "Let's first make a comparison."

Paulette left the dressing room and came bustling back a moment later with Daphne's dress. She held it up against Daphne and made

164

her stand beside me facing the mirror. "Remember what I said about the color? The cheaper dress looks yellowish by comparison. I just wanted you to notice."

"Maybe under the lights in the chapel," my mother commented, "the difference won't be so noticeable as under these fluorescents." She glanced up, squinting.

"And the neckline," Paulette pointed out, paying no attention. "Just round and banded, like a polo shirt actually."

"I like polo shirts," I remarked. "They look good on me."

"Well," Paulette said irritably, ignoring me and talking to my mother, "it's your decision, of course. If you really *want* the dress, I'll measure the hem for shortening. It will be ready on Friday."

Paulette knelt down to examine the hem. She looked up earnestly at my mother. "You still have time, though, to have the copy made up if you call me later today or early tomorrow. Just in case you should decide to speak to the older lady about it."

"We can't," I told her, looking straight ahead into the mirror. "See, she's fresh out of money right now, so we couldn't possibly bother her about it."

Paulette, still kneeling, made a last attempt to

get to my mother. "Children can sometimes be a little too sure of themselves. Grown-ups have to be the ones to make the final decisions about these things. A child can make a serious mistake. . . ."

There wasn't a sound coming from my mother. Oh, how I loved her! I looked down at the top of Paulette's head where the dark seams of her scalp were spreading into her red curls.

"Don't worry," I told the top of her head emphatically. "It's no mistake."

19 It was early the next morning, and Daphne was crying softly in her room. I wouldn't have heard her except that I was passing her door on my way to the bathroom.

On the way back, I stopped and listened some more. I was *sure*, this time, that the sound wasn't coming from the television set. For one thing, it was too early for soap operas and, for another, Daphne didn't watch the tube as much as she used to.

I knocked softly on the door and heard a stifled sob.

"What's up?" I whispered. "Can I come in?"

"Don't," Daphne called out in a panicky, choked voice.

"It's too late," I said, turning the knob and swinging the door wide open. "I'm in. Good grief, what are you doing?"

Daphne's flower girl's dress, which we had brought home from Paulette's yesterday afternoon, was laid out carefully on her already made-up bed. The wreath with the flowers and veiling rested just above it. Only the white shoes and stockings were missing. At the other

167

side of the room, Daphne, still in her pajamas, was hastily stuffing things into the smaller of her two suitcases.

"I'm going," she said, her back to me and her shoulders heaving with sobs that had now become noiseless.

I screwed up my face in confusion and disbelief. "Going where? You can't just get up and go back to California. You have to make a plane reservation. You didn't, did you?"

The back of her head shook from side to side to indicate that she hadn't.

"Well, where can you go then? Does my mother know about this? You must be crazy. You can't leave now. The wedding is only four days away."

Daphne swung around to face me. Her eyes were red and puffy. "That's just it. That's why I'm going."

"Why? I thought you wanted to be in the wedding. You have your dress. . . ." I glanced over at the bed. "What's it lying there like that for, anyway? It looks dead."

"It's for you," Daphne gulped. "If you take it back to the bridal shop today, she can make it smaller to fit you. She said she could."

"O-h-h-h—baloney. What are you talking about? I have a dress picked out. I got one I really like. Did you forget about that?"

Fresh, fat tears began to roll down Daphne's cheeks. Her entire body swayed back and forth as she knelt beside the suitcase. "You c-can't wear that dress you picked out. You'll s-spoil everything. It doesn't match. Paulette is right. Your g-grandma won't like it. Lainie won't like it. You'll see."

I plopped down on the edge of the bed beside Daphne's dress. "Oh yeah? So what? It's my body and I'll put it into anything I want. I said that I didn't like that dress on me, and I meant it. I think everything's working out just . . . great. You're the one who's spoiling things by making all this fuss. And just where do you think you're going anyway?"

"That's my business," Daphne retorted.

I was surprised at the way she spoke. "You know who you sound like? Shirley Brummage. The way she used to be. Hey, is that where you're thinking of going? To Shirley's apartment or to that Mrs. Ramirez, the super's wife? You might as well tell me, 'cause you won't be able to go now. I'll watch you all the time."

Daphne gave up trying to pack the suitcase altogether. She flopped down on the floor with her legs flung out in front of her and her back slumped against the wall.

"I should n-n-never have come here in the first place," she sobbed, between heaving sighs. "I could have s-stayed with a neighbor, a sort of friend of my m-m-mother's. But *your* mother was the one who kept insisting. She said you really wanted me. She said I'd be 'good' for you. But you didn't r-really want me, did you, Pamela? I knew you didn't all along. That's why I t-t-tried to stay out of your way right from the start." She dabbed uselessly at her eyes. "And now l-l-look what I've done. I've spoiled the wedding for you. Even if I swore to you that I didn't mean to, you'd never believe me. So I decided the only way I could prove it to you would be to go away, at least for a few days, until the w-w-wedding was over. . . ."

"Oh really," I said impatiently, to hide how rotten Daphne was making me feel, "that was dumb. It never would have worked." I leaned forward. "Look," I told her, "I'll level with you. I didn't want you to come. That's true. But it had nothing to do with *you*. I just didn't want *anybody* around. I knew it was my mother's idea all along. She had this thing in her mind about how I was spoiled and bossy and . . . and needed to learn to share with somebody."

Daphne didn't say anything. She just kept looking at me and choked back a big, dry sob like a hiccup.

"Okay, okay," I went on. "I am sort of spoiled

and bossy, I guess. Maybe I even take after Grandma Florence a little." I thought about that a moment. "Well, not too much, I hope. But maybe I do. Just a little. Anyhow, I don't mind your being here now as much as I did at first. I guess I cared a lot when Shirley Brummage seemed to take such a liking to you. But that . . . that's all right now. And it did really sting at first when Grandma Florence decided to make you a flower girl, too. But that's working out okay. . . ."

Daphne was shaking her head. "No, it isn't."

"Yes it is!" I insisted. "Don't you see? You get to be a flower girl—you know you really want to—and I get to wear what I want. If not for you, I'd have to wear that . . . that FG 3146 or whatever Paulette called it. So you're helping me out, honestly."

Daphne wiped her eyes on the sleeve of her pajamas. I got up from the bed and brought her a batch of fresh tissues. Her eyes and nose and lips were so swollen from crying that I wondered if she'd be looking normal by Sunday.

"You're only trying to be nice to me," she said, blowing her nose hard into three tissues. "Everyone's always trying to be nice. They don't really want to. They just think they have to be."

"Aw, come on," I urged, wishing I could get

171

her to stop gushing fresh tears every little while. "You're not so hard to be nice to, Daff." I'd never called her that before. "I know you think people like you only because they feel sorry for you or because you're pretty. But I'm sure lots of people really like you for yourself once they get to know you. *I* do."

She looked at me with a strange, disbelieving half-smile. I was afraid she was really going to start bawling. "Listen," I said quickly, "not that this has anything to do with what's happening now, but how come you couldn't have stayed in California with your mother this summer? I mean, how bad *are* things, really?"

The half-smile left her face. "Oh, bad. See, I couldn't stay at home because my mother isn't there in the first place. She's in a . . . a sanitarium, where she's supposed to get better. Only she isn't much better so far. She's there for . . . for emotional problems, you know, and drinking."

"Oh," I said, shocked. "I didn't know that she wasn't even at home." I paused, hating to go on. "But . . . but what about your father?"

"Well, he lives someplace else since he moved out last spring. In an apartment with a . . . another person. She's hardly much older than I am. Honestly. You just wouldn't believe it."

I shook my head. Now I *was* sorry I'd asked. But nobody had ever told me the details, not even Grandma Florence.

"It must be awfully hard for you to talk about it," I said to Daphne apologetically, after an awkward silence.

Daphne hung her head. "No, it's okay," she said quietly. "Actually, I'm sort of glad you asked me about . . . them. Because you'll have to know sooner or later. And . . . and I just didn't know how I was going to tell you, Pamela."

I looked at her in mild alarm. "Tell me what?"

"That . . . um . . . I'm not going back to California right after the wedding. That I'll probably be starting school here in the fall. . . ."

I fell back so hard on the bed that I actually began to roll over.

"Pamela," Daphne gasped, "be careful! The dress."

Daphne had already scrambled to her feet and hurried over to rescue the flower girl's dress, which I'd begun to crush. I jumped up and grabbed the dress off the bed.

Daphne was standing in front of me, searching my face. "So what do you think, Pamela?"

"About what?"

"About my staying here."

"Oh, that," I said, trying not to look directly into her eyes. "That's not . . . uh, too terrible. I sort of expected it."

I was still holding the dress, a smothering mountain of organdy and lace. All of a sudden, I pushed it into her arms.

"Here," I said, "for Pete's sake, take this thing and hang it in your closet so nothing happens to it between now and when you wear it. On Sunday."

I got myself out of Daphne's room real fast after that. I went into my own room and slammed the door.

"Not too terrible." It was terrible enough! I could see now that all my worries about Daphne staying with us forever and ever were almost sure to come true. No wonder my mother hadn't ever told me too much about her cousin Sandra and her problems. No wonder she'd been so furious with Grandma Florence for telling me as much as she had about Daphne's adopted parents.

One moment I hated Daphne for just existing and getting in my way; the next moment I felt sorry for her and even liked her. The moment after that, I hated the fact that I liked her, and

174

wished I could hate her. But how could I? She wasn't mean or spiteful. I'd tried to make her out to be. But I'd been wrong. That just wasn't Daphne.

My mind began to race. I pulled on some clothes and went out onto the upstairs landing. Daphne's door was closed again.

The door to my parents' bedroom at the other end of the hallway was open, though. My mother and father were downstairs and I could hear them murmuring softly to each other over breakfast. Had they heard us in Daphne's room? Had they purposely ignored us and gone about their business?

I wandered into my parents' room. I wasn't even sure what I was looking for until I saw it. There it was, a slip of paper lying on my mother's dressing table, the receipt for the dress we had ordered for me yesterday at Paulette's.

I examined the receipt carefully. The address and the telephone number of the bridal shop were on it. There was also a drawing of a formally dressed bride and groom, and at the bottom of the printed slip, in fancy lettering, it said: *Bridal Creations Unlimited.*

With the receipt in my hand, I tiptoed over to the bedroom door and softly closed it. Then I went to the telephone beside my parents' bed and dialed the number of Paulette's Bridal Boutique.

A thin, almost whining, woman's voice answered.

"Hello," I said, in my deepest, most grown-up, most sure-of-myself voice. "I'm calling about a white satin-polyester child's dress that was ordered yesterday by a Mrs. Teitelbaum. It was supposed to be shortened and ready for Friday."

"Just a minute," said the voice.

Just a minute for what? I glanced nervously toward the bedroom door.

The voice came back on again. "Okay, go ahead. What's the problem?"

"There's no problem," I said, firmly. "Just a message. Don't shorten it."

"Don't shorten it? Who is this calling, may I ask?"

"This is Mrs. Teitelbaum herself, of course. Who'd you think? The thing is, we're not taking the dress, even though we left a deposit, so don't shorten it. Got that?"

"Oh," the voice said, "I'll tell Madame Paulette. She isn't in this morning. Could I ask, please, what's the reason you're not taking the dress?"

"The reason," I said, clearing my throat several times while I tried hard to think of a good excuse, "the reason, ah, is that the child who was going to wear the dress has broken her leg and therefore will not be appearing in the wedding procession on Sunday."

"Oh dear," the voice said, "Madame Paulette will be very sorry to hear that, I'm sure. But, of course, as long as you've let us know in time, she will, of course, return your deposit. We hope the child recovers quickly."

"Oh, thank you," I replied. "I guess . . . uh . . . she'll get over it okay."

Then I put the receiver down very carefully, opened the door very gently, and went clattering down the stairs to breakfast.

20 There were a few short, warning blurps of organ music, and a hush settled over the rustling crowd of people that had assembled in the wedding chapel. I was jammed between my mother and father on a polished wooden bench beside the aisle. It was lucky that my wine-velvet party dress, which we'd pulled out of the cedar closet at the last moment, still fit me.

My father's hand patted my shoulder warmly. "Feel okay, honey?"

"Sure," I nodded.

My mother stroked my arm anxiously. "You all right, Pammy?"

"Course," I repeated. "What's all this? You're both acting like I'm sick or something."

My father chuckled softly. "You can't blame us. When Pamela Pieface Teitelbaum voluntarily steps out of the limelight—"

"Pieface!" I croaked in surprise. "How'd you hear about that?"

"Oh," my father answered, drumming on the back of the bench, "these things have a way of getting around. Anyhow, how can I help thinking of that Brummage friend of yours, with all the junk that's accumulating in and around my shed in the backyard?"

"Never mind about that," I told him. "Shirley really is going to get out of the hospital one of these days. And even if she can't go back in the junk business, she'll tell us where to sell the stuff for her and then she'll be able to buy something nice for herself with the money."

I sighed, just wondering what Shirley would have thought of the fancy wedding hall we were in. It had a bunch of different reception rooms and a great big ballroom with crystal chandeliers, curlicued gilt decorations, and thick, thick carpets.

"Well, anyhow," my father went on, "all this modest self-sacrificing withdrawal of yours . . . it isn't the easiest thing in the world to believe."

"It just isn't like you," my mother whispered. "We're afraid you might be having last-minute regrets."

"Nope," I told them both firmly, pressing my lips tightly together.

Just then the organ swelled into a sort of musical announcement and began to play a slow march to which the groom and his parents started down the aisle.

My mother nudged me. "Can you see all

right, Pammy? Here, change places with me."

We switched, and I moved into the aisle seat so I'd have a perfect view of the rest of the bridal procession.

Next, of all things, and to an even slower march, came Grandma Florence. She was all dressed up like a queen in powder blue and silver and was walking down the aisle all by herself, smiling and winking to the right and to the left of her. She certainly wasn't going to be left out of the wedding procession.

When she passed me, she actually blew me a kiss. I suppose it meant that she wasn't upset anymore about my not being in the procession, even though she had been at first. My mother and I had lied to her only a little bit, telling her—nearly at the last minute—that Paulette couldn't get the other flower girl's dress in my size and that we hadn't wanted to put her to the expense of having one made.

Near the very front of the chapel, in an aisle seat, sat Grandma Florence's friend, Herman, waiting for her to approach. He had a camera in his hands and, as Grandma Florence drew closer, he dodged nimbly out into the aisle and snapped her picture. Then Grandma Florence went on up the altar steps to stand under the canopy opposite the groom's parents, who were already waiting there.

The music got livelier and a little faster. Now came Lainie's mother with her arm resting on that of the best man. She, too, was wearing blue, but in a deeper shade than Grandma Florence. Then came the four bridesmaids, also in blue, and behind them the maid of honor, in a matching but fancier dress.

I craned my neck all the way to the back of the chapel to look for Daphne. She had to be next. The organ music had petered out and drifted almost to a stop, as Lainie's mother and the best man joined the others under the wedding canopy and as the bridesmaids took their places at the base of the altar, two on each side of the aisle.

Then, with a flourish of high-pitched notes, the music sprang up once again and swelled triumphantly into the wedding march.

I looked back again and there, at the beginning of the aisle, stood Daphne, a lone figure enveloped in a cloud of filmy white. Slowly she began coming forward, scattering creamy rose petals on the royal-blue carpet. Out of the throats of nearly two hundred admiring people rose a chorus of adoring a-h-h-h's.

Daphne *was* beautiful, with her flushed pink cheeks, her darkly fringed violet eyes, her rosy lips set in their dreamy smile. Her steps were small and perfect; her flower petals descended

181

in just the right places, never too many, never too few.

"Lovely. Lovely. Gorgeous child," people whispered. "Who is she? The bride's sister? Niece? Cousin?"

"Cousin"! I swallowed a lump in my throat the size of an egg, for sure. That could have been me. Should have been me. For an instant I hated Daphne all over again. And then her step brought her alongside the pew where I was sitting. She turned her head to look at me, and our eyes met. Her smile remained sweetly fixed. But, to my surprise, a single tear glistened on her cheek. And, just as she went past me, she blinked.

When Lainie herself came down the petal-strewn aisle, looking radiant on her father's arm, it was almost as I'd expected. There were hardly any more o-h-h-h's and a-h-h-h's for her than there had been for Daphne.

I glanced up at the crowded, canopied altar. Daphne was standing now with the rest of the important members of the wedding party, Grandma Florence among them, waiting for the bride to ascend and take her place beside the groom so the wedding ceremony could begin.

My mother put her arm around my waist and squeezed me to her. "She did do it nicely, didn't she, Pammy?"

"Who?" I asked, pretending I wasn't sure who she meant.

"Daphne, of course. I mean, well, she really was a credit to all of us."

I nodded. "Sure. I knew she'd be great at it."

My mother put her head very close to mine. "Tell the truth, Pammy. Did it hurt very much?"

"Nah," I said, feeling another egg-size lump swelling in my throat. Or maybe this one was only going to be the size of a very large grape.

"Anyhow," I added, "the next time, it gets to be my turn. And *I* get to do my act alone. Daphne understands about that. I made a deal with her."

My mother gave me a baffled look. "What deal? What next time?"

"When Grandma Florence gets married, of course."

My mother clapped her hand to her mouth just in time to stifle an outburst of laughter. "Oh, Pam," she said in a choked whisper as soon as she could talk, "you really are too much. I never thought of that."

"Sure," I whispered back. "Why not? You didn't think I'd changed *that* much, did you? And, anyhow, this sharing stuff is supposed to work both ways, isn't it?"

My mother brought her head even closer to

mine. "The point is, though, you made a *deal*. You weren't making deals a while back, as I recall."

"Okay," I agreed. "So I did. Even Shirley Brummage says you never know when you might need a friend. She told me that when I saw her in the hospital. I never thought I'd hear a loner like her say that."

There was a solemn chord from the organ to get everyone's attention. A tall, bearded man in black religious robes stood towering over Lainie and Elliot, sternly facing the audience in the chapel.

My father leaned over past my mother and poked me gently. "Sssh, quiet now, Pieface. The ceremony is about to begin."